THE WAITING PLACE

a novel

Amber Wynn

COPYRIGHT

CHRISTOPHER RASHAD GLOBAL ENTERPRISES, INC.
Copyright © 2017 Amber Wynn
All rights reserved.
ISBN-10:0-9980856-0-X
ISBN-13: 978-0-9980856-0-9

Cover illustration by Amir Williams

DEDICATION

This novel is dedicated to all the beautiful girls who don't know that they're beautiful . . . who have lost their way because of hurt from their past, and fears that keep them so bound to their present they have no hope for the future. I hope you find your compass that lies not too deep inside you; and that you'll let it guide you to the treasure that is you. Once centered, you'll realize that you're enough just as you are, and you won't lose your way. The places you go will be the places you chose to go, and not the places you end up as a matter of circumstance.

ACKNOWLEDGMENTS

Oh, The Places You'll Go! is a children's book written and illustrated by Dr. Seuss by Random House in 1990. It was the last book published in the author's lifetime, one of the top ten Dr. Seuss books of all time, and a favorite gift bestowed graduates as they transition into the workforce.

The book concerns the journeys of life and its challenges with the narrator telling the reader that the world is their oyster and that they should make the most of their time. It serves as the backdrop to this story, illustrating how decisions shape the future of three college graduates.

This novel emerged as a collaborative effort between me and my beautiful sister gurl, Keisha Brown (now Keisha Wright). It was originally a treatment we submitted to the Ben Affleck Matt Damon Green light Project – that wasn't selected to advance to the finals.

I'd like to thank Keisha for agreeing that I should turn this into a novel (with the provision that if it ever gets a movie offer, she has first dibs at the screenplay. But, of course!) But mostly, I'd like to thank KB for sharing in one of the most amazing writing journeys two sisters could share. It was a very revealing and bonding weekend.

I love you, gurl!

Table of Contents

PROLOGUE

The Choices You Make . . .

August 10, 2017 5:30 p.m.

"Inmate H-70780, chow time!"

A narrow metal rectangular window slides open. I move to the massive iron door and grab the tray: one slice of wheat bread lies on top of cold instant mashed potatoes and watered-down gravy. In the right corner, a red apple, the left, a Dixie cup full of red Kool-Aid with no sugar.

I place the tray on the floor next to the twin bed; lay back on the paper-thin mattress covered by a worn grey wool blanket, and turn to count the days on the calendar. I've spent thirty-eight days in confinement while my paperwork is being 'processed' into the system.

Seven more days before I'm transferred to general population. Seven more days before I can receive approved visits. Seven more days before I officially begin my fifteen to life sentence.

Someone gave me a Dr. Seuss book when I graduated from NYU, but I never understood the significance of it until recently. In fact, I never even read it for the longest time. Now as I sit here, certain parts of the book just pop into my head . . .

Like, *'You can get all hung up in a prickle-ly perch . . .'* and something about *'your friends will leave you and, you'll be left in a lurc*h' . . . and *'out there things happen, and frequently do, to people as brainy and footsy as you*[1] *. . .'*

I pause, taking in the cramped space around me. Then in my best Dr. Seuss voice, I say, 'I'm sorry to say, but sadly it's true, that bang-ups and hang-ups can happen to you.[2]'

It's amazing, the things you remember when you have a lot of time on your hands But I'm getting ahead of myself. Let me start at the beginning . . .

---

[1] Dr. Seuss, *'Oh, The Places You'll Go!'* verse 13
[2] *Ibid*, verse 12

CHAPTER ONE

. . . The Path You Take

Congratulations!
Today is your day.
You're off to Great Places!
You're off and away![3]

Monica Lopez

June 1, 2017   *10:00 a.m.*

It's an unseasonably warm spring morning in New York. The sun's rays have turned the once spectacular peak fall foliage of muted orange, yellow, gold, maroon and red leaves into a sea of green street trees from fifty-two different species that line crowded Washington Square in New York University's School of Law.

As I make my way down the congested street as a recent NYU graduate, I can barely contain my excitement. Twenty-two, the world ahead of me, I am filled with this overwhelming sense of anticipation about what's next in my life.

I'd done it. I'd humped and pushed and made it through college. The first in my family to do it. I had big plans.

Ignoring the stares from passersby, undoubtedly trying to decipher my ethnicity, I cut through the hustle and bustle of the crowd and the New York energy that weighs heavy on everybody's shoulders, slowing down the communal pace.

---

[3] Dr. Seuss, *"Oh, The Places You'll Go!"* verse 1

As the sun gently makes its appearance, I continue into the NYU Law School building. NYU commencement banners hang motionless from buildings, stifled by the rising heat.

On display in the lobby of the Furman Law School building are oversized black and white photos of people in high places who have fallen from grace at one time or another.

Sponsored by the Center for Research in Criminal Justice, the title of the exhibit is *Acts of Betrayal*. Focused on my point of destination, I walk through the lobby and pass the life-sized pictures of Bill Clinton, right hand raised, taking the Presidential oath. And then a picture of him, right hand raised, testifying before Congress in the Monica Lewinsky trial.

I walk pass a picture of OJ Simpson from 1968, as a USC Trojan in the infamous Heisman pose; and then one of him in court holding his hands up in the famous leather gloves.

Then there's a picture of Marion Berry – in a dark blue, three-piece suit as Mayor, and then again as an inmate, dressed in prison blues. Next, is a picture of Mike Tyson holding his championship belt high above his head, and another of him cuffed and headed off to prison for rape.

Up to the left is a picture of Jim Baker with his wife on a crusade preaching the word of God; and then a picture of him in tears, begging his Lord and congregation for forgiveness of his transgressions.

But I only glance at the photos hanging from the ceiling by fish wire as I continue decidedly to my destination, the final grade roster.

I push my way through the crowd of students gathered around the Introductory Formal Logic course grade sheet. I slide my sunglasses down the bridge of my nose, looking over them to scan the roster for my grade. I find my social security number, and trace my finger across the 8.5 x 11 sheet of paper from my number to my grade: 98%

I smile—more than satisfied with the final grade for my first law prep course. I am doing everything I can to ensure I succeed. My professor said learning how to symbolize and analyze logical statements and arguments would help me become a better law student and lawyer. This Introductory Formal Logic course focused on that, and how to think in a linear and organized fashion.

With purposeful strides and a fast-pace, I push my way back through the crowd of students and set off for my next destination.

§ § §

I walk through the large double doors of the law school and accidentally bump into a white sorority girl -- blonde, with huge boobs that fill out her Kappa Kappa Gamma sweatshirt. That blonde Bitch tries to give me attitude as she sizes me up.

"Excuse you," she says.

"Bitch, excuse you!" I say, giving her a light shove. I pause and wait for her to respond. She gasps as if she can't believe I would have the audacity to touch her, but she doesn't say a word and certainly doesn't swing on me.

I look at the Bitch like, *that's right, Bitch, keep it moving!* And walk past her and out the door.

I guess she's not used to seeing a Boricuan from Spanish Harlem on this campus. But I am here, fought hard to get here, and ain't going to let no sorority girl or anybody else keep me from what I have dreamed about since seventh grade.

Fifth born of a family of six: three girls, three boys. Puerto Rican mom, African American dad. The Lopez's live in a four-story railroad apartment. The Suarez family lives on top, Sra. Rodriguez lives on the second floor, and my family lives in an un-renovated three-bedroom on the third floor.

I'd lived in Spanish Harlem all my life. Couched between two sisters in a full-sized bed, I don't know what privacy is. My outside world closely mirrors my inside world—apartments, stacked tightly next to and on top of each other. No space, no breathing room. Just crammed together, sucking up all the precious air they stole from the city. My sisters, Annabel and Marisol stole the air from our room.

My parents, Yolis and Victor share a room, my three brothers share a room, and my sisters and I share a room. The living room is a constant thorough way of bodies colliding into each other.

With two older brothers and two older sisters, I've mostly gone through life unseen. Manuel, my oldest brother, is twenty-six years old and has given my dad a run for his money--in and out of jail. Roberto is twenty-four years old and isn't too far behind, getting caught up in the True Money Gang. Raul is the youngest, seventeen (an oops baby) and I see signs of restlessness in him, too.

Annabel, my oldest sister, age twenty-five, is the worst. She's been running the streets since elementary school when she first started ditching. Mama beat her black and blue so badly the fucking social workers came to the house.

"¡Perras!" Mama screamed, "Estoy tratando de mantener su culo en la escuela! Voy a vencer al diablo de ella o morir de mierda tratando de." The neighbors, and probably half the block, heard my mom calling them all kinds of Bitches. She told them how she was trying to keep her ass in school; and, how she would beat the devil out of *her* child, or fucking die trying, to make sure she did!

My mom is one hundred percent Puerto Rican, and one hundred-percent buffet catholic. She picks and choses what aspects of Catholicism she practices depending on the situation. She is typically really devout right around the times my brothers go to jail.

Mi abuela on my dad's side was African American and his dad was Puerto Rican. But his dad was so dark; Papi came out looking one hundred percent Black. His thick curly hair is big and full and his nose wide and thick. Unless you heard him speak, you seriously wouldn't know he was half 'Rican.

Marisol, age twenty-three is quiet. But it's true what they say; it's the quiet ones you have to watch. That Bitch would sneak off and hang out with her boyfriend, Jesus, the asshole trying to jump Beto into True Money. She ended up pregnant and in Job Corps.

I am the first to graduate college in my family. My Papi was so proud. My mama cried through the entire ceremony. I just shook my head at the bunch of them, screaming and acting all banchee. I finished NYU in four years. And my parents never paid a dime in tuition.

"¡Mi hija es muy inteligente! Obtuvo una beca por cuatro años. Dicen que no son los genes González?" Yolis bragged about how intelligent I was, getting a scholarship for four years. She was quick to give the Gonzalez gene pool credit.

What Yolis didn't know was that my college education was primarily funded compliments of Sin & Seduction Gentlemen's Club. I'd always been a fabulous dancer. I learned quickly how to parlay those skills into moneymaking opportunities.

What my mama didn't know wouldn't hurt her. I got that degree; everything else is irrelevant.

Monica

June 1, 2017   *10:00 a.m.*

On a busy New York street in the Village, I watch as Jacky sashays her way through the crowd. Boss runway walk, bad-Bitch attitude parted the crowd like Moses parting the Red Sea. Several feet behind her is Camille Coleman, her best friend, who is being pushed back and forth by the crowd like a metal ball bouncing in a pinball machine.

The two are physically opposite. Camille, a light skinned African American is timid, homely, and lacks the easy assurance Jacky's semi-sweet chocolate flawless street smarts afford her.

Camille follows Jacky down the street.

"Moni! . . . Moni!" Jacky shouts above the crowd. She waves her arms wildly above the masses to try and get my attention as she continues her easy stride in my direction.

Camille drops her camera and a file of black and white photos splatter across the street. Camille bends down to collect her things, and ends up dropping more than she manages to pick up.

Jacky yells again, a little louder. "Monica Lopez!"

I smile and wave over the crowd in the direction of the familiar voice. We finally lock eyes; Jacky smiles and makes her way over to me.

"Jacqueline Roberts!" I yell back.

I meet eyes with Camille not too far behind Jacky, trying to catch up, and lose my smile. I greet Jacky with a warm hug and give Camille a weak ass wave.

We pull apart. "What's up girl?" I say to Jacky.

I turn to Camille and give her a fake smile. Camille shifts her stuff to her right arm and scratches her left arm.

"Hey," I say to Camille.

"Hi," Camille replies.

Jacky rolls her eyes at us and shoves a department store bag into my hand. "What's up? This is for you . . . in celebration of your graduation and everything," she says smiling.

I pull the black Armani pantsuit out of the bag.

"Ooh!" Camille says.

"Ooh!" I scream. "This is hot!" I say smiling at Jacky.

"Save it for your first trial," she says.

I hug her.

Jacky turns to Camille, "And this is for you." She hands Camille a box.

Camille almost drops it trying to open it. It is a black leather portfolio for her photographs. It has her name engraved on a shiny silver plate on the front.

Camille replies, "Thanks Jac. It's beautiful."

"Bitch, that's a thousand dollar portfolio!" she says. "Uh, some enthusiasm, please!"

Camille scratches her left arm absentmindedly.

"Oh, I'm sorry Jac. I love it! I swear I do. It's just . . . my parents are driving me crazy!" She makes a face and mimics her parents, *'Camille, we think you should do this. Camille, we think you should do that.'* You'd think I just graduated from elementary school and not college," she says exasperated. She looks down and strokes the portfolio. She looks back up at Jacqueline. "They're stressing me out."

I chuckle. "Why don't you guys come to the club tomorrow night and release a little stress?"

Camille frowns and I suck my teeth.

"You know Camille doesn't like the club," Jacky says.

"Why, not bougie enough?" I say folding my arms across my chest.

Camille squints her eyes at me. "No, that's not it at all," she says.

"Come on, Cam, it'll be fun!" Jacky pulls Camille into her side.

Camille pauses. "Is Marcus coming?" Camille asks.

I roll my eyes at Camille. "Maybe."

"Does it matter? Let's just go and have a good time. My treat," Jacky says.

"Ooh, aren't we the big spender today?" I say.

We all break out into laughter.

"All right. Give me the address again. I'll ditch the Colemans and see you guys tomorrow," Camille says.

I search my Gucci tote for a piece of paper. I find a shiny black business card and scribble the address of the club on the backside.

"Here, the address is in black. Just ignore the stuff written in blue. I can't find anything else to write it on."

Camille takes the card and throws it in her purse.

"Okay, see you tomorrow night then?"

"Yes, of course you will." Jacky laughs.

I turn to Camille. "See you later, Cam."

"See ya," Camille says.

I hug Jacky again. "Congratulations, graduate!" I say to Jacky.

"Congratulations to you, Counselor!" Jacky says.

"Uh . . . not yet . . . I've got to *finish* law school first." I laugh.

"You will. You've worked too hard not to become the most famous black female lawyer there is," Jacky replies, her eyes sparkling.

My heart warms as I embrace her. "Thanks. You've always been in my corner," I say looking into my friend's eyes.

"I'll always have your back. You are, after all, my girl—right?" Jacky smiles.

Camille snaps a candid shot of the two of us embracing.

"Right. Always," I say grinning.

Jacky was different. She sat next to me in English class on her first day at LaGuardia. Christy and Jeanette were trying their hardest to get up in her space – it was so obvious. I even think Jacky knew, but she blew them off, which low key made me so happy because they were the Bitches who gave me the most shade.

Even though nobody really fucked with me because of Marcus, nobody went out their way to be my friend either. I wasn't no punk, so I walked around campus like I didn't need no friends; but the truth was, I wanted some.

In walks, Jacky, in her Dereon jeans and Louis Vuitton backpack, shoulder-length hair bouncing like she just left the shop. The girls sat up and postured as she made her way to the back of the class. When she walked past them their mouths dropped.

"Can I sit next to you, Morena?"

"Who the fuck is Morena? My name is Monica Lopez."

She smiled as she took her seat next to me. "My bad. I meant it as a compliment." She tossed her hair over her shoulder. "*Monica Lopez!*" she repeated.

We laughed.

She turned to Jeanette who was gawking. "May I help you? Shit, you're weirdin' me out." She looked at me and rolled her eyes as if to say, *what the fuck is wrong with her?*

From that day on Jacky and I were connected at the hip.

I couldn't quite figure out why. Christy and Jeanette were more like Jacky than I was. They were from upper Manhattan. Rich, uptight Bitches from well-educated families who thought they were better than everybody else. But Jacky never acted like them. Never.

I used to go over to her house all the time. She had the most amazing bedroom ever. It was the size of our entire apartment. Her walk-in closet was the size of me and my sisters' bedroom. She had a sleigh bed that was so high off the ground she had a step stool. She had six huge yellow and white pillows that matched a beautiful yellow bedspread she called a duvet. It was the most beautiful thing I'd seen— straight out of a magazine.

My bed had a hand me down quilt from my grandma on my Papi's side. It was like five hundred colors from all the mitch-match patches sewn together. I used to love it because my Papi loved it. But being wrapped in 'years of history' didn't feel as good as being swaddled in an eighteen hundred-count thread duvet.

My favorite thing in Jacky's room was the vase of fresh flowers that sat on her nightstand next to her bed. Every week she got new ones. Sunflowers were her favorite so most times there were six huge sunflowers in a heavy square clear vase. They made her room bright, happy.

We talked about everything: boys, them triflin' heffas at school, our parents, siblings . . . our futures. Jacky was going to marry a baller. She talked about it all the time. She was so beautiful and confident, nothing in my mind thought it wouldn't happen.

The first time I take Jacky to my house, I am so embarrassed. Beto is trying to push up on her and my sisters throw her so much shade, I think I am going to have to fight my own people.

But she just smiles like she doesn't see any of it. Instead, she ooh's and ahh's over my mom's food like it's the best thing she's ever tasted in her life.

"Mrs. Lopez!" she says, sipping the hot roux from the chicken gumbo. The only American dish she makes better than any American-born that I've tasted. "This is sooo good."

My mom beams. "Thank you, preciosa." She wipes her hands on her apron. To me she says in Spanish, "I like this one. She's got a good head on her head. See, it was a good thing putting you in that school, prieta. You making friends with good girls." She smiles at Jacky. "And she got money."

I am embarrassed. But I am so happy to have a friend, I just agree with Mami. "Si Mami, Jacky is a good girl."

Jacky winks. And every birthday and Christmas she buys my mom a name-brand purse.

At first my mom balks and says it's too expensive. But after the women in the barrio make such a fuss over the fact that she could afford a *real* designer purse with all them kids, she can't wait to show off the new piece envy. And Jacky never disappoints. The purses are always fabulous.

17

"You know you're creating a monster?" I say to her after the third purse. "She gets seriously offended if anyone accuses her of having a knock off. She looks down her nose and be like, 'This ain't no knock off!' and shows them the label."

Jacky laughs and claps her hands.

"Yes, like a true fashionista!" She seems genuine when she says, "I love seeing your mom happy." Jacky smiles, "Every woman should have something in her closet that makes her purr."

I think she got pleasure from being the source of the few smiles that fought their way on Yolis Lopez's face.

What Mami didn't know was that every one of those purses, while real, came from Jacky's hook up, *Back of the Truck, Chuck*. Chuck boosted everything from designer purses to top sirloin steaks, from Rolex watches to True Religion jeans. You named it, he got it.

I never told her, though. I loved Jacky and needed Mami to love her too. If she knew her shit was stolen, not only would Jacky never step foot into her house (a house Jacky could probably pay cash for with her trust fund) again, but she'd have me in on my knees in church every day and would probably move me to another school.

Now that I had a road dog, I was cool with being at LaGuardia. Having access to all her hook ups were just perks that made being Jacky's friend even more special.

CHAPTER TWO

Don't It Always Seem to Go,

You Don't Know What You Got til It's Gone?

"So be sure when you step,
Step with care and great tact.
And remember that life's
A Great Balancing Act." [4]

Jacqueline Roberts

June 2, 2017   *4:30 p.m.*

It's busy inside the crowded Macy's department store where I've worked my last year in college. I run an American Express card through a card reader at my register. As I wait for the machine to process the request, I can see my customer checking me out.

My straight, shiny, black, shoulder-length hair is pulled high in a sleek ponytail. I'm rocking a rag and bone sweat suit with Black Christian Louboutin Escarpic spike pumps, and conspicuously large diamond studs.

The look is all money—and I have the perfect body to pull it off. Long, lean torso; full double D breasts, and hips and ass to match.

The reader flashes APPROVED. I hand the card back to my customer who smiles broadly. I wink, step from behind the counter and hand him two large bags full of merchandise.

---

[4] Dr. Seuss, *"Oh, The Places You'll Go!"* verse 31

I turn to Evelyn and Sandra, my co-workers and toss my hair. "Well ladies, that was my last swipe as a Macy's employee! You be sure and have a nice life now," I say.

"You'll be back," Sandra says.

"Only to shop, sweetheart. Only to shop!" I reply.

The girls laugh. Evelyn shakes her head.

I follow the male customer out of the store and over my shoulder as I wave goodbye I say, "No offense ladies, but it's time for this NYU graduate to find herself a real job."

🎩🎩🎩

In the security camera above, undercover officers watch Jacqueline's last transaction from beginning until she exits the store. As she walks out the door, a female undercover security guard walks behind Jacqueline's register, punches in some numbers and prints out a copy of the last transaction.

🎩🎩🎩

In a high-rise co-op in the upper Westside, I apply the last of my make up, *All that Glitters* in quick short strokes in the front corners of my eyes. *Bronze* dabbed in the center. And *True Blue* applied in an outward contour toward the outer corners. MAC shadows applied to accentuate what more than one man has called long sexy Bambi-shaped eyes. Next liner, and then finally the mascara.

"Are you ready?" Jasmine says as she saunters into my room. Clothes are tossed everywhere. Bags and shoes line the walls. Jasmine Navarro is my girl. Even though she's only twenty years old, she is hellah cool. We've been friends for four years: I was a sophomore in college, and Jasmine was in her senior year in high school when we first started hanging out. Jasmine had just broken up with my younger brother, Andre, who she busted playing on her with a Boricuan from the Village.

The Bitch wasn't even cuter than Jaz; she just had a big ass. At first, Andre was very vocal about his displeasure with us being friends, but got used to her being around after a while—had to, we quickly became close friends and have been inseparable ever since.

Jasmine is a petite and curvaceous Filipina with long auburn hair that touches the tip of her bra strap.

Stepping in front of me, she grabs a brush, tosses her head to the right, and vigorously brushes her hair.

"Bitch! Hello – Mirror?" I say, shoving Jasmine, who laughs.

"Uh, hello yourself, Bitch, you're supposed to be ready!" She walks over to my dresser and sprays herself with a gush of my Coco Channel.

"Yeah, that's not toilette water, Bitch. You don't need to drown yourself."

Jasmine rolls her eyes and replies in Tagalog, "Ako ay mula sa isang ikatlong mundo bansa, hindi isa pang kalawakan - Alam ko ang pagkakaiba sa pagitan pagbibihis tubig at parfum."

"English, Jen Mei – English!" I shout.

"I'm from a third world country, not another galaxy - I know the difference between toilette water and parfum."

I give her the bird.

"Fock you, Jock-leen Ma-rie! Fock yooooooou!" she says in her most Asian accent.

Although she is two years younger than I am, Jasmine is solidly in the same league in terms of goals and ambition. We both want fame. And we are both convinced that we can quickly get it by hooking up with someone rich and famous.

Some might say we are one hundred percent certified groupies who chase after the glamorous life. But we feel we were much too refined to be considered groupies. We are both beautiful; we spend hours getting our fierce on, always wear name brand, in-season fashion. And we only date men who can afford to keep us laced in the fashion we have become accustomed to.

Most of my friends consider me an oxymoron: daughter of a high-powered, partner in a major law firm — my mother; and CEO of a Fortune 500 for a father--affluent African-Americans who are well educated and well bred—as my grandmother would say, "Respectable Money." Yet, here I am, hob-knobbing with the nouveau riche and trendsetters.

By all accounts, I have the pedigree that positions me for a charmed life. Despite my upper middle class breeding, you won't find me in any country club or sorority step show. As one of Manhattan's hottest socialites of the Paris Hilton, Kim Kardashian echelon, you'll find me frequenting the latest celebrity hang outs (Sugar Fish, Catch, The Vnyl, The Spotted Pig in NYC)—where I am always waved in, having been on the arms of numerous athletes, I am easily recognized.

People, US, Vibe, E!TV and TMZ are some of my sources for the latest celebrity updates. I am constantly on social media (Facebook, Snap Chat, Twitter), reading blogs, watching videos, and I know every letter of every class of every luxury car (C-class for Mercedes, I-Class for BMWs) and what features distinguishes them.

I study eat, breathe, and sleep celebrity life. Being a part of that environment comes as natural to me as walking in five-inch heels. The way I speak of celebrities makes you think I know them personally, "Girl, did you see that hair piece Tyra had on at the Grammys?" I'd say to Jaz, "I *know* Greg, her hair stylist had to have been at the London opening of Sasha's where she featured that front lace hair piece," I'd say rolling my eyes. "Girl, with all that forehead, that style would work perfectly for her." I'd laugh. "It's a shame all that attention went to that tired blonde lace-front wig when it should be going to those beautiful new breasts Dr. Kolker just gave her, shit!"

Looking at my upbringing, most don't quite understand my obsession with celebrities and that lifestyle. I can't explain it either, really. Attending the best schools, participating in extracurricular activities, associating with other business-track upper middle class families, you'd think I'd be on-track for the same conservative lifestyle.

My parents were married young. My mother, DeLena, made partner in five short years. She spent long hours winning cases and building her career. That's why my dad, Charles left her – she rarely spent time at home with the family.

My mom has always been a great mom. Honestly, I've never wanted for anything. And with her bankroll, I've never worried about being able to afford anything. Some say I'm spoiled--I say I'm well taken care of. *Tomayto, tomahto!*

I realize it was my mom's way of making up for her absence. And I've always been good with it. Not everyone has designer sunglasses, shoes, and clothes at their fingertips. I've always said, 'These things come at a hefty price.' For some of my friends whose parents are very involved in their lives, they didn't have material things to the degree that I did. But on the flip side, I've always had hardworking, *absent*, parents. The payoff is material things.

With their combined incomes, the Roberts have a comfortable lifestyle. A co-op in Upper Manhattan. A Tesla for my mom, a Range Rover for my Dad. Comfortable . . . *and flashy!* Haters said. Who do they think they are Bill and Claire Huxstable? The perfect little Black family – successful attorney wife, CEO dad, prep school daughter and son.

It did look perfect. On the outside. But there is no such thing as perfect. And even though I grew up adored by my doting mother, and loved deeply by my father – I have to admit, something was missing inside the beautiful Jacqueline Marie Roberts. And it wasn't intelligence. I graduated summa cum laude from NYU. It wasn't looks; I've always gotten compliments on my beautiful café au lait complexion, hair past my shoulders and hourglass figure. I have admirers no matter where I go.

But something was missing. And it was this missing that set me on my path.

Jacqueline

June 2, 2017   *6:30 p.m.*

Jasmine tosses her cell in her Kate Spade Dark Cildro Pink hobo purse. "Jared is waiting for us downstairs. Our reservation is at seven." She reaches inside her matching make-up bag, retrieves her Sapalicious lip lacquer by MAC, turns to face the mirror and apply a hefty layer on her full voluptuous lips. "You ready?"

"What is he driving?" I ask as I give myself a quick look over in the full-length mirror, running my fingers through my hair. I tuck my white baby doll BCBG t-shirt down in my low-rise True Religion jeans. I slide into my three-inch floral patterned Jimmy Choo pumps.

"The LR3," Jasmine replies as she pulls her breasts up out of her Victoria Secret Very Sexy push up bra, exposing more cleavage. She adjusts them so they are standing up looking perky. She smiles.

"Oh, hell yeah! Let's go," I squeal grabbing my slate blue Balenciaga handbag.

"What up, mama?" Jared says.

Jasmine sticks her head through the driver side window and kisses him on the lips.

"Damn, you look hot!"

"Thank you," Jasmine says, tossing her long straight hair as she strolls around the front of the car.

"Damn!" he says, looking at me. "You rockin' them stilettos!"

I smile, place my hands on my hips, and point my right foot out. He steals a quick peek at my ass as I round the back of his truck.

Jared is a baller. Jasmine is his tailor. And she custom-makes his suits, shirts, and pants. Her services include designing his clothes, packing and shipping them to whatever city he is in for a game, and unpacking and pressing his suits for pre-game. She'd lay out his outfit, and if he wanted, helped him get dressed. The only item he is allowed to pick out to wear is his underwear. Everything else Jasmine meticulously coordinates. Post-game, she packs them up and ships them back home.

She is 5'4"; he is 6'7". Standing, she comes up to his navel.

When you're horizontal, height is a non-issue, Jasmine would say. *'Shit, when you're vertical, riding that dick, it's a non issue as well.'*

Jasmine tried to break into the business the traditional route, but never got any contracts. Her designs are exactly the same: the only thing that has changed is her services. If a baller wants her to travel to the games, he pays her handsomely, six thousand dollars round trip. Of course, that means she stays in his penthouse, ready to respond whether he beckons or calls . . .

But she gets perks as well: she eats at the best restaurants, gets floor seats at the game, and gets into all the hottest clubs. If the baller has a woman at that game, she gets her own suite, and spending allowance (usually an additional three thousand).

"My Ina always say, *'Why give away pussy when you can charge for pussy?'*" Jasmine says to me one evening over drinks.

"Yo mama says that?" I say, with a scowl on my face. DeLena would never say such a thing.

Jasmine stares into her glass, then slowly takes a sip.

"My mama had three husbands; each one richer than the next. That Bitch didn't play when it came to her paper."

"Damn, three husbands. She must have had some bomb ass pussy," I say.

Jasmine looked at me, held up her glass, and we burst into laughter.

"To working that pussy, Bitch!"

"To working that pussy!"

Jasmine was discreet with her sexual indiscretions. Of course the players talked. But she never confirms anything. She's been in the business three years now and has a roster full of players she designs custom suits for. She has gained enough legitimate business to where she only sleeps with a few of her clients. Usually the players from the very beginning who helped her get paying contracts. Brian always gets love. He is the one who told a TV reporter who commented on how sharp he looked that Jasmine Navarro was his designer.

Once, a rookie was trying to push up on her and she checked him hard and low.

"What's up, lil mama? I need some *alterations* on this piece right here," he said, holding his dick in his hand.

Jasmine turned and looked him in the face, turned back around and grabbed her garment bag.

"What you *need* is some psychiatric help. You must have fell and bumped yo head, nigga. I ain't the one." She walked out.

Her motto is, "My pussy, my world. I always have choices."

While she questions a lot of things in life, she is sure about that one thing. And after giving her all to my brother, Andre – her loyalty, her time . . . her heart, only to be kicked in the face, Jasmine decided to take a different route this time around. It would not include giving up the heart--maybe a little ass. But no one is allowed into the sacred place that could be shattered into a million pieces. Been there. Done that.

This route means Jasmine is in the driver seat. She will allow herself to like a man, but never fall in love. The most damage that could happen would be a fender bender; she is over the three-car pile up that happened as a result of falling in love.

I love the lifestyle Jasmine has given me access to. Hanging with athletes, getting access to VIP parties, and hobnobbing with the rich and famous.

Jasmine loved him. Hell, she *still* loves him. I am confident she'd take him back if he *looked* like he wanted to ask her to get back together. But he will not. Andre is on another page. The chapter is called 'Uncommitted'. And it is dog-eared on "All about me."

I love my brother, but he has just gotten his swag and is on the road to sowing every oat in the field. Jasmine will have to wait a long time before he will be ready for an exclusive relationship.

In the meantime, I feel Jaz is doing the right thing: banking her chips and living life. And oh what an amazing life she is living. I'm just happy to be her friend at this time in her life. I truly care for Jasmine, but the truth is having a friend with over twenty NBA athletes at her fingertips is the best shit ever!

CHAPTER THREE

The Good Child

"You have brains in your head.
You have feet in your shoes.
You can steer yourself
any direction you choose." [5]

Camille Coleman

June 2, 2017   *7:00 p.m.*

Camille Coleman, second child born to Clarisse and Cornelius Coleman. I am named after my dad's mother who killed herself when he was nine by jumping off the George Washington Bridge during rush hour traffic. That should tell you something about me. Like, why would you saddle a perfectly innocent child with the name of someone who simultaneously took her life and ruined yours by jumping off a bridge?

I'm a middle child, born unceremoniously two years after my dynamic sister, Candice (Candi) and two years before my bratty brother, Cory.

In my mind, both my parents are unconscionable: Clarisse, an event planner, caters the crème de la crème parties and events. She has an "A" list clientele. In her early beginnings, she started as an assistant for one the industry's most well-known caterers, Christy Brennigan, of Christy's Couture Creations. After hosting several successful parties for my father, she quickly obtained notoriety and a client-base that

---

[5] Dr. Seuss, *"Oh, The Places You'll Go!"* verse 2

launched her into her own successful event planning business affectionately named after the daughter she adores *Candi-liscious*.

My dad began his career as an actor but took a part-time job in a casting office. And, as he describes it every opportunity he has a chance to tell the story, *fell in love*. Today, he's one of the top-casting directors on Broadway, having found talent for more than fifty shows on the Main Stem as well as television series, commercials, and films including *Seinfeld, Sex and the City* and *Friends*. Despite the economic downturn, he never felt the impact. He was working as much as ever.

Sinners. Insufferable. Adulterous. Weak. Sinners: the description of my parents from the perspective of a middle child--a middle child who lives in the shadow of Candice Annemarie Coleman, actress, fashion queen, wild child. The child they could not control.

Candi was a cheerleader—when she wasn't getting suspended for fighting, ditching, and making out with boys in the stairwell. She kept my parents busy. They were elated when she graduated high school and was accepted into the Wood Tobé-Coburn School for fashion and merchandising, an accelerated program where she could obtain a degree in ten to sixteen months, which was important because Candi couldn't stick with anything too long. I'm confident she is ADD.

And the ADHD kid is Cory: the last of the bunch. A busy body since he dropped out the womb. I remember being dropped at the neighbors' regularly because my parents were rushing Cory off to Emergency. Once he was running with a pencil, fell on it and punctured his chest. Then he got a cherry pit lodged in his ear. Another time he got sick from eating or drinking (I'm not sure which) a bottle of Elmer's glue.

I've always been the quiet child, the good child. The child who always did well in school, and 'never gave her parents trouble.' It was a stigma that worked both in my favor and against me. Right now, it is working against me. I want to pursue a career as a photographer, but my parents want me to pursue a career with more substance.

"We allowed you to major in liberal arts, and minor in photography with the understanding that you would select a career that would offer you some stability," my mom says. "But photography is a hobby, not a career."

"Unless you plan on working for National Geographic or some scholarly journal," my father says. "And if that's the case, I'm happy to reach out to a couple of colleagues to see if they can help you obtain an apprenticeship with the magazine." Cornelius looks at me over his horn-rimmed glasses.

"Or, how about I decide what I want to do with *my* future?" I say. "Since, after all, it is my life we're deciding on."

"Camille Marguerite Coleman!" my parents shout in unison.

"That is disrespectful. I did not raise you to speak that way to your parents," Clarisse says.

I cross my arms over my chest and plop down in the chair. "You did raise me to have an opinion. And you raised me to fight for what's right," I whisper, looking down at my feet.

My parents look at each other. "We just want what's best for you," my father says.

"I know, Dad. And I want what's best for me. And I love photography. What could be better for me than doing what I love? Isn't that what you've always told me? 'Do what you love and you will never tire of doing it.'"

My father smiles, "Yes. Yes, of course. But we want you to be able to take care of yourself, Camille, not live a life of famine or feast. Most photographers do not have steady incomes."

"That's not the life we want for you," Clarisse says.

"Then it's settled? I have no say so in my future? Clarisse and Cornelius have spoken. And so it is."

I stand and run for the stairs.

"Camille!"

"Don't worry about it, Mom. I'm the good child. I'll do whatever you say. Heaven forbid I have a thought of my own. A passion that I actually want to pursue."

Detective Morales

June 2, 2017   *10:55 p.m.*

"Oh shit!' I close my eyes and lay my head back on the headrest.

I focus as the pressure builds up.

Damn, it feels so good.

Just as I'm about to pop one off, I feel moisture on my dick. I jump, yanking a hand full of hair back.

"Ouch!" Miko screams.

"What the fuck are you doin' bitch?"

She looks up at me through dark sunken eyes.

"Just trynna make you feel good--"

"I told yo crack head ass I wanted a hand job!" I shove her back and grab a t-shirt from off my back seat and wipe off my dick.

"You used to love my blow jobs." Miko slides back into the passenger seat.

"Yeah, well that was before you stopped being selective about whose dick you put in your mouth." I reach into the inside of my jacket and pull out a baggie with three rocks in it.

She watches my hand like a cat watching a mouse, ready to pounce.

"I shouldn't give you shit. You fucked up my nut."

Miko quickly grabs my dick in her hand.

"I gotchu. No worries. You gone bust a nut tonight daddy."

Bright ass high-intensity headlamps damn near blind me as a black Mercedes sedan whips around and jackknifes into a parking space across the street.

Miko slowly works her magic. "Oh yeah. That's it. Shit yeah. Right there."

Once again, I feel the pressure rising. My dick is rock hard.

Miko works my shaft like a pro: up and down and really fast over the tip. She does this over and over. The pressure intensifies. My dick is throbbing. Miko tightens her grip around my shaft and strokes. Fast. *Mmm.* Faster. *Oh.* This shit feels so got damned good.

"Ahhhh!" I grab the steering wheel, oozing all over her hand in pulsating throbs.

Damn. I remember when my shit used to shoot ten feet.

I look down at the thick jiz. I remember when it used cover a majority of the front windshield. Miko grabs the t-shirt and wipes my juices off her hand and my dick.

"How was that?" She says eying the plastic in my hand.

I hand her the rocks. She smiles, revealing decaying teeth.

I don't fuck Miko anymore. Not since she started *looking* like a crack head. Her Japanese and Black features used to complement each other: big ass, small tits, those slanted eyes, and long, straight black hair that I would wrap around my hand pull tight before I bust a nut. Now her face is sunken and all pocked up, her body is skin and bones. But her hands – she gives the best hand job in the Bronx.

Miko is out the car before I can zip up my pants. Skipping her tweakin' ass to the crack house to get high as fuck off those three rocks.

I get out of my car, put on my leather jacket, and walk over to the black Mercedes.

CHAPTER FOUR

Leaving My Mark

"You'll get mixed up, of course,
as you already know.
You'll get mixed up with many
strange birds as you go." [6]

Marcus Williams

June 2, 2017   *11:00 p.m.*

Outside the strip club, I pull my Mercedes CLK to the curb. I turn off the engine and turn down the blaring rap music.

Monica sits frozen in the passenger seat. She grabs her Gucci bag from below her feet and reaches for the car door handle, but I grab her arm, yanking her back toward me -- preventing her from opening the door.

"What?" Monica shouts.

"I don't get a kiss?" I say.

Monica thrusts her left cheek toward me, while rolling her eyes. I plant a soft kiss on her face.

"Don't be like that, girl. You know I love you. Don'tchu?"

Monica slides on her Gucci sunglasses and opens the door. She slams the door shut and storms into the club.

"You break my shit, you gone be spinning extra hard on that pole to get it fixed! Shit."

---

[6] Dr. Seuss, *"Oh, The Places You'll Go!"* verse 31

I watch her disappear into the red brick building. I can't control the smile that forms across my face watching that bubble bounce as she walks. The men in the club will drop dollars just to have her jiggling that ass a few minutes in their face, but that right there, that's my ass. Mine, 24/7.

As I slip off deep in thought about my girl, I feel a tap on the shoulder. I damn near jump out of my seat. I turn to see fuckin' Detective Morales all up on me. Fucking Puerto Rican fuck!

"Man, you can get fucked up walking up on me like that!" I shout at his ass.

The corners of Morales' mouth inch up to form a smirk. He takes a long drag on his cigarette and slowly exhales. "What you got for me?" he says through the lingering cloud of smoke.

"It's coming!" I say, tugging on my jacket.

"It's been coming for quite some time. How long do you think I'm supposed to give you?" Morales says taking another puff.

"Man, I'll have your shit tomorrow."

"No! Tonight. Not tomorrow. Tonight," Morales says. He straightens up, and starts to walk away. He takes a long drag on his cigarette, flicks it toward the gutter, and walks back to my car.

"And don't fuck with me!"

Morales walks off, back in the direction he came from. Once he's clearly out of sight, I sit up and curse a couple of times.

This muthafucka is all up in my ass! I can't wait to move this shit, get him and a bunch of other marks off of me. They think I can't deliver. But once this shit goes down, him and the rest of them fools gone see.

I'm the youngest of four boys: Malcolm, Martin, Mandela, and Marcus. Despite being raised by Miss Bernadette, a God-fearing woman, with civil-rights DNA running all through her veins, we all manage to turn out the opposite of our namesakes.

Malcolm was a major player in Billy Guy's (Maryland's infamous drug kingpin) four million dollar dynasty. A New York-based lieutenant, Malcolm was wiring Guy a hundred and twenty-five thousand a week from his South Bronx cocaine and heroin sales. Martin and Mandela were Malcolm's most ruthless street dealers, instilling fear in their competition across state lines.

Moms was heartbroken. All the things she fought against: crime, drugs, and oppression—her boys capitalized on.

Malcolm pleaded guilty to conspiracy and smuggling charges. In exchange for the plea, prosecutors dropped kingpin charges against him and agreed to recommend a ten-year prison sentence without parole. Martin and Mandela's cases are pending.

Ten years younger than Mandela, I still live in the shadow of the notorious Williams Brothers. Because of my brothers' past, my moms is all up in my shit. I've been called handsome and funny, but that shit don't help you on the streets. I am a Williams brother and will get my due respect once I establish a name for myself. Which happens to be the perfect opportunity for Detective Morales.

Five years on the Brooklyn North Gang Squad landed him a promotion to Detective with the Seventy-fifth Precinct. With him come his connections to the hustlers, corner lookouts, and shot callers in the neighborhood. Morales approaches me looking for inroads with my brothers' drug cartel. Two weeks ago, he hands me two kilos of cocaine that never made it to the evidence room. And now he is back to collect.

In an attempt to 'steer me down a different path', my moms rode my coach until he pulled some strings, called in some favors and got me transferred to Fiorello H. LaGuardia High School to play on the baseball team.

She had done her research. LaGuardia offered tuition-free accelerated academics to city residents. She refused to take money from my brothers who would have made sure my tuition was paid. So, getting me into this school was her solution.

It's at LaGuardia where I meet Camille, Monica, and Jacqueline.

Marcus

September 10, 2012   *8:45 a.m.*

"Good morning, ladies and gentlemen."

"Good Morning Miss Brayden."

"We have a new student joining us today," she says, looking over her bifocals to read the paper. "A transfer student, Mister Marcus Williams." She looks up at me and smiles.

Some busta in the second row leans forward and whispers in his homey's ear loud enough for everyone to hear, "Mister Marcus is rockin' some bomb ass bubble gums!"

The entire class bursts into laughter.

"What's so funny?" Miss Brayden demands. She bangs her hand on the desk. "Now see here, if you don't stop that right now I will send each and every one of you to detention for an entire week!"

The room quiets down to hushed mumbles and snickers.

"Never mind them," she says, smiling at me. "Some people just don't have good home training." She points to an open seat in the middle row. "Go take your seat right over there next to Camille. Camille, raise your hand, please."

Camille raises her hand. Me and the pit in my stomach make our way pass the rows of snickering kids over to the peculiar looking girl. She is pretty underneath the thick red-rimmed glasses and poofy bangs.

I sit and stare down at my sneakers. They called them bubble gums. I don't know what bubble gums are, but I know from the way everyone reacted they aren't fashionable.

My mother had depleted most of her savings trying to keep a roof over our heads. She refused 'Blood Money' from my brothers, so life was rough in the Williams' household. I even tried to get a job, but she refused to hear of it.

"Your job is to go to school, get good grades, and make something out of yourself!" she'd say.

But after today's humiliation, I knew without a doubt I would be doing whatever I could to make money. I had to tighten up my gear.

"Pull out a pen and some paper. It's time to journal," Miss Brayden announces.

Embarrassed, I realize I don't have any pens or paper.

Camille slides five pieces of notebook paper and two pens on my desk.

I look over at her. She smiles. It was the most beautiful smile I'd ever seen.

During lunch Camille shows me around campus. She takes me to the cafeteria, the library, the main office, and the quad—where each class level hangs out, and where the jocks, nerds, and cool kids kick it.

I tell her about running track, so she shows me where the track and field and gym are.

"Don't worry about Jason. He's a prick," Camille says as we leave the track and field.

"I'm not worried about that busta."

"Okay, good. He's not worth your time. He gets off on making people feel bad about themselves because he feels bad about himself."

"Why do you say that?"

"I've gone to school with Jason since kindergarten. His mom is on drugs," she says softly. "He stays with his grandmother most of the time because his mom is in and out of rehab, or jail – or wherever the courts make her go to keep her kids."

I listen. I act as if the information she's sharing about my mortal enemy means nothing, but inside, I'm smiling from ear to ear.

Three weeks later, I roll up on my brother's homeboy Tony.

"What up, T?" I say, giving him some dap.

"What up, son?"

"Yo, check it. What can a soldier do to hold some paper over here? For real tho, son." Tony looks me up and down and bursts out laughing.

"Yo son, take yo square ass home to yo momma." He turns his back on me.

"Oh, it's like that? You really gone front me like that when Malcolm is still running this shit?"

Tony turns around and looks me up and down. "You got some heart. You is a Williams Brother ain't you?" He chuckles.

"Damn straight. And I'm coming to you real, son. I need to get me some kicks. Look at these shits my moms got me wearing."

Tony looks at my shoes and falls back covering his mouth and starts laughing. I stare him down. Tony straightens up and coughs into his hand.

"Awe damn, son. Yo moms is on some real shit, though. She got yo brothers threatenin' the whole crew. We ain't supposed to fuck wit you, lil man."

I stand there thinking. "I hear you. I ain't trying to get you caught up or nothing. But on the real, I need you to show me some love." Tony looks me up and down. "What size you wearing?" He scans the area, like a deal is about to go down. "I ain't never about to send a pimp out looking like a Bitch. That's not how the brotherhood works in this borough."

"I wear a size nine."

"Aiight. Hold up." Tony pulls out his phone and walks off. Fifteen minutes later, he returns with a dark green trash bag.

"Hear yo go, G," he says with a crooked smile. "They ain't new, but they clean. They should fit you."

I give him a hug. Tony hugs me back.

"I'ma tell my brothers you looked out for me, T. For real, son. And you know, whatever you need . . . . Whenever you need it, I'm your soldier."

"Get yo ass out of here before Mrs. Bernadette be digging in my ass," Tony says, turns and walks off.

Before I make it to the next block, I call Camille on my cell.

"Hey, I want to show you something," I say. I try to contain it but I can't. I know my voice is full of excitement.

"Okay, come over." Camille texts me her address.

I take the subway to her exit, and walk the rest of the fifteen minutes to her house in a hellah nice area of Tribeca.

"Hey," Camille says, opening the door.

"Hey back," I reply, suddenly feeling self-conscious about the green trash bag full of clothes and shoes I was once so eager to share with her. I hesitate.

Camille turns around. "Well, come in." She smiles.

I walk in, close the door and take in the opulent home.

"Um. Is. Is it okay for me to be here? I mean, where are your parents?"

"Yes. It's okay for you to be here, silly." She grabs my hand and takes me up the stairs to her bedroom. "They are in 'the industry'," Camille says using air quotes. "They don't usually get home 'til way after eight, most times even later."

Camille's bedroom walls are lined with photos. There were pictures of everything from her family, to rain drops hanging off a rail on an abandoned brownstone. There are pictures of random scenes: people sitting on the subway, kids jumping through a spray of water at a broken water hydrant, a dog pissin' on a tree. They were the most amazing photos I'd ever seen.

"Holy shit!" I say, turning in circles, trying to take it all in. "Who took all these?"

"I did," Camille whispers.

"Holy shit! I'm best friends with a fucking genius!"

Camille beams. I study each photo. "Wow!" and "Man, this is tight!" and "Dang, Camille, you're so talented."

I spend an hour going through all of her albums, listening intently as she explains the reason why she took the shot and what it means to her.

"Enough about me. You sounded so excited when you called. What is it that you want me to see?"

I had forgotten about the green trash bag. I had waited to open my treasure with my new best friend. I'd never had one before and over the last three weeks, spending time with her every day, talking to her, sharing my deepest fears and greatest aspirations in life had felt like the white cream on top of my mom's red velvet cake, pure perfection!

After seeing her house, and her room, I suddenly feel . . . less than.

"Awe nah. I'm cool. I was just . . ." I can't find the words.

Camille walks over to the green trash bag, picks it up, and hands it to me. "Show me what's in the bag, Marcus. Stop being a fucking retard."

That was the first time I'd ever heard Camille curse. My laugh loosens the tension I feel in my throat.

"A fucking retard, huh?" I say shoving her.

She shoves me back.

"Yes. Don't get all weirded out because of this." She waves her hand around. "It's not mine. It's not me." She lowers her head.

I lift her face so her eyes meet mine. "This is yours. It is you."

"No. It's my parents'," she says. "These photos, these are me."

I understand. I certainly would have preferred to live in Manhattan over Brooklyn, to have my parents' house look like this versus my mom's one-bedroom apartment. I don't feel like that is me either. So I understand what she means.

"I see you, Camille Coleman." We stare into each other's eyes. "I see *you*," I say again and kiss her.

I can tell she's shocked at first, but the warmth and softness of my tongue sooth her. I had never thought of Camille in that way. But now that my lips are on hers, I can't imagine her any other way.

I pull away. She opens her eyes and blushes.

"Okay, so I got this stuff . . . and I wanted to show it to you."

"What is it?"

"I, I don't know really." I hesitate. "I think it's clothes and shoes. Man, I was so excited I didn't look. I wanted to wait and check them out with you."

Camille smiles broadly. "Then open it up! What are you waiting for?"

I open the bag and pull out at least four pairs of damn near new sneakers.

"Oh my god, Marcus!" Camille screams. "These are Jordan's!"

I smile. Camille's genuine enthusiasm gets me hyped. Knowing her parents can afford to buy her a dozen of those and more, but she is excited for me, touches me in a place I didn't know existed.

"Try them on. Here, with this shirt. Oh! Now try them on with these jeans. Yes, those go really good together."

I strip down to my underwear right in front of Camille. She blushes but keeps looking. I try on at least a half dozen outfits. After the second outfit, Camille grabs her camera and starts taking pictures.

"Pose for me. You're the model on GQ magazine."

I strike a pose. We laugh. She clicks. I pose. She clicks. Then finally, I take off the clothes, excited about my new wardrobe. I stand in the middle of her room in just underwear.

Camille is sitting, watching me.

I turn to face her and see how intently she is watching. Something stirs inside me and my dick starts to rise. Camille's eyes grow big. Intrigued by her fascination I move in closer to her.

"Do you want to touch it?" I whisper.

Camille doesn't reply.

"Have you ever touched a dick before?"

She shakes her head, and looks down. I feel so much warmth toward her. I gently lift her face, and kiss her soft and slow. She kisses me back--slowly, then with more eagerness. I take her hand and slide it inside my underwear. She takes my dick inside her moist hands.

I close my eyes. She slowly strokes it up and down. I pull down my draws. My dick pops straight up. Camille jumps back.

I open my eyes, grab her hand and gently kiss her palm. Then I kiss each finger. I can hear her breathing. I sit on the edge of her bed, and move her hand down to my dick and wrap her fingers around the shaft. I slowly move her hand up and down, and increase the pace. My mouth falls open; my breath grows shallow with each stroke.

After about ten minutes of stroking, I explode. I grab her covers on either side of me as she continues to stroke my throbbing dick. The warm juices shoot across the room, the remnants ooze out and down her hand. It is the most amazing thing I have ever experienced with a girl.

"Do you think I can take a picture of that next time?"

I laugh out loud. "Negative, Ghost rider!" I sit up and look into her eyes. "Do you want there to be a next time?"

Camille nods. Her eyes are glistening, and a huge smile covers her face.

I quickly go from the embarrassed boy with the bubble gums to the bad ass you never want to cross. Three weeks after Jason's crack, I am stepping on his neck in my almost new Jordan's.

"Jason. You like my new kicks?" Jason gasps for air. "I can't hear you. You like my new kicks? Since you didn't like my bubble gums. Are these up to your standard?"

Jason coughs, gasping, grabbing at my shoes.

I swing hard and sock him in the face. "Don't. Touch. My sneakers." The kids point and stare at the blood oozing down Jason's face.

From that moment forward, nobody ever dare laugh at Marcus Williams.

I go over Camille's house every opportunity I get. Her parents are rarely home, and her siblings seemed to have plenty of after school activities that kept them away from home, too. It's some wild shit, I can't understand. If I lived in a beautiful home like that, I'd for sure always be there.

When Camille's little brother, Cory is at home, I keep him occupied by bringing my X-box over for him to play all the latest games.

It gets to the point where he waits at the door for me to arrive just so he can jump on the game and get to the next level of whatever game he was playing last.

Meanwhile, in Camille's room, the two of us explore every inch of each other's bodies. Camille has become obsessed with the amazing sensations I am able to make her body experience with my fingers . . . and now, my tongue.

I am amazed at the number of orgasms she experiences in one afternoon. She has honed her skills in hand masturbating, and is more than eager to move to oral sex.

She's shared with me that she used to sneak into her father's porn stash and look at the pictures in his Playboy and Penthouse magazines. When she found his videos she would lay spread eagle and touch herself while watching the porn stars *boom chica bow wow*.

"Can I make love to you?" I ask Camille one afternoon.

She freezes.

We are lying naked in her kitchen, licking whipped cream, melted chocolate and honey off each other.

"It's been a year, Camille," I say. "We've done everything there is to do except penetration. I don't know about you," I caress her wet pussy, "but I'm ready for the next level."

Camille closes her eyes as I slide my fingers expertly in and out of her oozing wet and warm walls. I know exactly where to touch to make her cum. I watch her face and increase my speed as she increases her gyrations. And just before she's ready to cum, I pull out.

She looks flustered. Shocked. "What? Why did you stop?"

"I want you. I want to make you cum, Cam. Did you hear me? I want to make love to you," I say to her.

Camille slides over and kisses me long and hard. She strokes my dick and it instantly grows hard. She smiles, and then slides my dick inside her mouth. She sucks and slurps and takes me inside her with the same expertise. I start to pant as I feel my juices making their way to the head of my dick. She sucks and sucks.

I push her off. My juices ooze out the top of my dick. She goes to lick it, but I stand up and walk away.

"What's wrong?"

"You know what's wrong? You're ignoring me."

"I'm not ignoring you. I'm trying to please you."

"You can please me by letting me cum inside you. I want to feel you. Be inside you."

Camille stands up. "I can't, Marcus." We stare at each other.

"Why not?" I say. "We've done everything but penetration, what's the difference?"

"That is the difference. I'm a Christian. I can't have sex before I'm married. I just can't. I'm sorry."

"Are you kidding me?" I say, pacing back and forth around the kitchen. "Camille, you don't think what we've been doing for the past year is sex?"

"No, of course not!" she says. "I'm still a virgin."

"Girl, ain't shit about you a virgin." Camille looks away.

"You know exactly where your g-spot is. You know exactly where to put my finger to make you cum. You know how to suck a dick better than any strawberry in Queens. You can jerk my dick better than I can – and it's my dick!"

She turns her back to me. I walk up behind her, wrap my arms around her waist.

"Camille. I'm a man. I can only do this for so long. I love you." Camille turns to face me. She throws her arms around my neck. "I love you, too!"

"Sex is what two people do when they love each other."

"Sex is what two people do *after* they are married."

I stare into her eyes, shake my head, and pull her arms from around my neck.

"Ok Camille."

I pull on my pants and shirt and walk out the door.

🎩🎩🎩

I don't visit Camille for two weeks. At school, we hang out like normal. But I refuse to go over to her house.

"I miss you," Camille whispers in my ear one day at lunch. We're sitting on The Green underneath a sycamore tree. She slides her hand on top of my dick. I move it away.

"I miss you too, babe," I say. "But I can't keep doing that. It's too hard on me."

"It's not like you have blue balls, Marcus. You cum, too."

"Yup. But I want more."

"I can't give you more. You know that."

"I know you say you love me. But you tease the shit out of me."

"That's not fair, Marcus. I'm not teasing. I'm . . . I'm trying to make you happy without compromising all of my morals."

I just look at her. "Well, I'm going to help you keep all of your morals. How about that?"

Senior year brings with it a defining moment for me and Camille. I love her, and can't stay away. I suffer through sexless months, settling for the release Camille provides with her hands and mouth.

But one day, a storm blows in from Spanish Harlem that changes everything between me and Cam. Her name is Monica Lopez.

CHAPTER FIVE

Boricua Morena

"You're on your own.
And you know what you know.
And YOU are the guy
who'll decide where to go." [7]

Monica

September 7, 2013   4:00 p.m.

Life changes for me the moment I step foot on LaGuardia High School of Music & Art and Performing Arts. It's the only specialized public high school that does not require art, dance, music and theatre applicants to take an admissions test. Instead, students are accepted through auditions; New York's way of offering inner city youth access to quality education.

Good for me because I suck at standardized tests. But I kick ass at my audition. I have them standing on their feet clapping when I finish.

And here I am. At LaGuardia: twenty thousand students take the test and nine thousand audition this year. Only six thousand one hundred six students are offered admission—and I am one of them!

LaGuardia could have as easily been Disneyland—even though it is located in the Lincoln Square district of Upper West Side Manhattan—it is a world beyond my world.

Now I am at this school with the rich kids who have their own beds, in their own rooms, who rock only name brands, and speak

---

[7] Dr. Seuss, *"Oh, The Places You'll Go!"* verse 2

perfect English. They walk, talk, and act like money. And here I am, youngest of the Lopezes . . . first to leave Spanish Harlem to go to school. I'll be the first to get my degree. My JD to be exact!

First step: attend a good high school.

Check!

I make it in, but I never *fit in* LaGuardia. The way I talk, the way I dress—I see how the Manhattan snobs look at me. I ain't stupid. I peep it all. The cool kids, the nerds, the Goths they all have cliques, and I don't fit into any of them. They certainly don't extend an invitation.

I also observe how nobody fucks with Marcus Williams.

"What up yo?" I say to Marcus just as he is walking off the field after baseball practice one day.

"What up, Boricua?"

I am wearing black knee-length leggings that accentuate my butt and a neon green muscle shirt over a black sports bra.

"I was wondering if you wouldn't mind showing me around this place."

"Didn't they give you a tour during orientation?' Marcus says, bending down to remove his cleats.

"Yeah, but I keep getting lost. They went so fast, I don't know which building is which." I undo the ponytail that sits on top of my head, unleashing the full head of curls that, after I shake them loose, cascade down my back.

Marcus smiles. "Yeah, sure. I can show you around."

"Cool. Thanks. Let me know when you want to do it."

"I want to do it now." He says, tossing his bag over his shoulder. "You available?"

"Yeah. Sure. If now works for you, it works for me."

CHAPTER SIX

The Power Move

"And then things start to happen,
Don't worry. Don't stew.
Just go right along.
You'll start happening too." [8]

Marcus

October 12, 2013   *4:00 p.m.*

Monica is a new dance student transferring from East Harlem. I've seen her before. I sat in the cut and watched her audition. I knew she'd get in. She is good—powerful, precise, and full of energy. There were ten other girls on the floor that day, but she was so captivating, they were like background noise. She stole center stage that day.

I try not to look surprised when Monica approaches me and asks for a tour of the campus. But I am; females on this side of the track are not usually that forward. But she is, and she's comfortable with it, which makes her intriguing. As we walk across campus, I get an up close look at her. She's absolutely stunning.

---

[8] Dr. Seuss, *"Oh, The Places You'll Go!"* verse 7

I show her around upper campus, then lower campus; pointing out to her the same things Camille showed me a year ago. I end by showing her the back entrance to the dance studio.

"Do you have time for me to show you something?" Monica says.

"Yeah." I follow her into the dance studio.

Inside, she puts on a CD, walks to the center of the room and goes down on one knee, head lowered. As the music starts, I watch Monica transform into this amazing mass of energy. Although she's thick, she's fluid and limber, and light on her feet.

Her routine isn't like the last one I'd seen. Today, her movement across the hardwood floor reminds me of an athlete on track and field: smooth, agile, and coordinated.

This choreography is slow and melancholy. I feel the sadness, the rage and power in each move. It is a beautifully arranged piece—a mix between ballet (with the perfectly executed turns and kicks) and modern dance (running, jumping, leaping, and fluid movements). I am entranced, feeling her intensity with every move she makes.

When she's done, I am so filled with emotion I don't know what to do. She turns to face me. I stand and clap and then ceremoniously bow.

"Don't make fun of me," Monica whispers.

I walk over to her, turn her to face me.

"I'm not making fun of you. I am bowing because you are fucking amazing. I am . . . in awe."

She stares me in the eyes. I do not blink. I pull her into me and we kiss: a long, deep, hungry kiss, and another, and another.

Monica pulls my shirt over my head. I pull her muscle shirt over her head. We kiss as we move down to the floor. I slide on top of her and pull down her pants. She watches as I remove my track shorts. I am half expecting her to pump the brakes, but she doesn't. Instead, she spreads her legs to receive me and closes her eyes as I slowly enter her. The sensation is so mind blowing I can hardly believe it's happening to me.

We pull mats down to the floor for the next two rounds, and christen every corner of the room. Afterward, we lay quietly on the floor entangled in each other.

"Do you have a girlfriend?" Monica says, looking up into my eyes. "I guess I should have asked before I had sex with you . . ."

I chuckle. "No, I don't have a girlfriend."

I feel a twinge of guilt after I say it. Technically, I've never asked Camille to be my girlfriend, but for the past year and half I have only spent time and been intimate with her.

"Would you like one?" She swings her leg across my torso, mounting me. She slides back and forth across my dick enticing it to grow hard. I quickly respond. Monica's face registers sensuous satisfaction as she grabs me, slides me inside her and begins to ride me hard.

"Oh fuck!" I scream. "Yes. Yes. Will you be my girlfriend?" I whimper.

Monica smiles.

The weekend comes and goes, and on Monday, Monica walks onto campus with a new sense of belonging.

Everything changes once people see us cuddled up on the quad.

Camille

I watch them from inside a classroom. I snap a picture of them, why, I don't know. Because the image of them boo'd up had already been forever emblazoned in my mind. I overhear a classmate talking about them.

"You know Marcus and Monica are together now, right?" the girl says.

"What? Since when?" the other girl replies.

"Since--look over there at them lip-locked, swapping spit."

The girl gawks, looking out the window across the quad.

My eyes remain fixed on Marcus and Monica cuddling under a tree. They're so close and familiar. Marcus rubs Monica's lower back. Monica rests her head comfortably on his shoulder.

I know, like everyone else, that they are having sex. I don't hear the girls speculate about it because all I can hear is the thunderous sound of my heart shattering into a million pieces.

CHAPTER SEVEN

The Boom Boom Room

"Somehow you'll escape
all that waiting and staying
You'll find the bright places
where Boom Bands are playing." [9]

Monica

June 2, 2017   *11:10 p.m.*

Inside the club, I plop my bag down on a chair in front of a vanity mirror. I pull off my sunglasses and stare at a blackened right eye. I slowly unbutton my blouse, looking in the mirror at the dark green and purple bruises on my chest and neck.

I pull out my small make up bag and begin to cover my bruises with MAC make up.

The hot, humid New York air sneaks its way into the muggy club, causing the air conditioners and bartenders to work overtime.

There she go sliding down the pole
There she go sliding down the pole

---

[9] Dr. Seuss, *"Oh, The Places You'll Go!"* verse 22

"That's right!" the D.J. says into the mic. "Let's bring 'em out, bring 'em out!"

The intro to E-40's *Sliding Down the Pole* signals the roll call. About twenty girls in all hues, ages, shapes, and sizes fill the stage.

"Awe shit! Here they come."

Mae Mae, an anorexic-looking Asian with hair past her ass crosses in front of me. We call her iHop, because that Bitch is as flat as a fucking pancake, but she be making it rain.

Trixie, the oldest dancer of the group, does a slow, deliberate walk to the front. She leans over and jiggles her double D's in front of her regulars. They go wild.

Trixie is old as shit, but just as her name says, she be doing some kinky ass acrobatics – climbing to the top of the pole, stretching her legs out, touching the ceiling, then swinging around the pole, all the way down to the bottom, where she flips, then hits the floor and bounces up and down two or three times. She's old, but she got all kinds of tricks that keep 'em coming.

There are some Halle Berry, Kim Kardashian, and Ariana Grande look-a-likes, but all they got is looks. They couldn't dance if Jesus cane down from heaven and asked them to.

"Niggas, hold on to them woodies. Y'all ain't seen nothin' yet!"

We dance across the floor getting the club amp'd.

"Aiight! Aiight! I can see some of y'all burning holes in ya pockets." He Laughs. "I gotchu, Playa, right there in the purple button down, looking like Steve Urkel and shit."

The guy turns to look at the D.J.

"Aiight, aiight. Don't be mad doggin' me and shit. I'm just havin' a little fun. I'm a old head. Y'all in these big ass glasses and Poindexter looking outfits--" He steps back and starts laughing. "Nah, I'ma stop. I'ma stop. Just for you, my brotha, cuz I'm clownin' and shit—I'ma give you the Blue Light Special!'

The guy in the lavender button down pumps his fist in the air.

"Yeah!" he says, and moves in front of Raven, a Nicki Minaj look-a-like with ruby red hair—correction, lace front wig. She squats and spreads her legs wide.

"That's right! Sin and Seduction's very own two for twenty special!"

The D.J. scratches and changes the song to T Pain's *I'm In Love with a Stripper*. We all bounce, grind or wiggle extra hard.

"There it is! Your anthem, baby. It's why you're here. Come find your bae and get them two dances for twenty dollahs."

The men move to the front of the room. "It ain't gone last long. Y'all betta stop tryin' to be cool and get up here and get this Blue Light Special!"

The music plays for about a minute. Some of us leave the stage and work the room.

"X'Stacy, come to the stage."

I finish my dance and head over to the D.J. booth. I tell the D.J. my song and head to the center of the stage while the rest of the girls clear the room.

The first eight beats of Rihanna's *Wild Thoughts* bellows out from the club's speakers. The funky guitar of Carlos Santana's 2001 hit, *Maria Maria* gets the room going

"Hey!" a female raises her hands, snaps her fingers, and dances in her chair.

I take my place in the center of the dance floor on the main stage. Kevin hits the spotlight, which illuminates all my curves in a sexy silhouette.

"Gentlemen!" The DJ says, hyping up the crowd. "Pull out your tens, twenties, fifties—cuz this ain't no one dollar bill booty. OG's set your pacemakers to low because taking center stage is Sin and Seduction's sexiest chocolate hottie!"

I open with a steamy acrobatic dance, wrapping my legs around the pole and slide down into a sexy wide-legged split as the lights change from red to blue to orange. The crowd goes wild as I lean back and slowly lift my legs up and out into a wide 'v', giving a full view of my black satin-lined vagina.

"Gentleman, pimps, and playas!" The DJ says. "Put your hands together and help me welcome Sin and Seduction's very own X'stacy!"

I don't know if you could take it
Know you wanna see me nakey, nakey, naked

I work the pole with ease. An older Caucasian man dressed in an expensive single-breasted navy suit waves a hundred-dollar bill in my direction.

I slither over to him and thrust my cleavage in his face. I mesmerize him with the fullness of my ruby red lips. I mouth the chorus, seductively telling him that when I'm with him all I get is wild thoughts.

The man smiles, places the hundred between my breasts, and returns to his seat. I wink at him and he winks back.

Camille

June 3, 2017   *12:45 a.m.*

I wait for two guys to enter the club and sneak in behind them. Jacky texted me saying she'd be here by 12:30, but I don't see her and it's dark in the parking lot. I don't feel safe. So I pay and inch into the seedy club.

As I round the bar, I see him. *Marcus.*

I can't help but get giddy. He still makes my heart race after all this time. I grab my charm and rub it.

Stop it. I say to myself, running my hand over my hair and adjusting my skirt. I lick my lips and slowly make my way over to his direction. But Marcus' eyes are fixed on the stage. I turn to see Monica bent over, jiggling her butt in some man's face.

I pull out my phone and snap a profile picture of Marcus smirking as he watches Monica's performance from the bar. He removes the toothpick hanging out of the corner of his mouth and points it toward Darryl, an oversized bartender, signaling him to come over. The buff, bald black man makes his way over to Marcus who raises his glass in the air for a refill.

Marcus never once takes his eyes off Monica, and fails to notice me standing beside him. Darryl pours Marcus another shot of

Hennessey. Marcus downs the shot, licks his lips and signals for another.

Monica leads a gentleman in a navy suit into the Champagne Room. He follows behind her, all smiles. I watch Marcus glare at the two until they're out of sight.

Marcus raises his glass once more. Darryl slowly shakes his head.

"Fuck you!" Marcus screams.

Drunk and angry, Marcus reaches over the bar for the bottle of Hennessy. Darryl grabs Marcus' forearm and twists it behind his back. He pushes Marcus away from the bar. Marcus loses his balance and stumbles.

I help Marcus up as he spits incoherent venom at Darryl.

"Marcus, why don't you get the fuck outta here," Darryl states more than asks.

Marcus turns to face Darryl; he pulls his black leather jacket behind his hip to reveal the handle of a Glock 9 tucked inside the waist of his pants.

"Are you asking, or telling?" Marcus says, stumbling back and forth.

"Marcus . . ." I plead.

Darryl laughs at Marcus and walks to the other end of the bar. I try my best to hold Marcus up, but he has ninety pounds and one foot in height on me. I struggle to keep him from falling.

"Please Marcus, let's just go," I say.

Slurring, Marcus says, "See, ain't no nigga gone tell me when it's time to go. Only a fine ass Bitch like this can tell me when to leave!"

I ignore Marcus' backhanded compliment and wrap my arm around his waist. I can't help but bend from his weight. With his arm around my shoulder, his breath hot on my neck, I lead a stumbling Marcus around the bar.

I plop Marcus up against the wall and rumble through my tote to find my car keys.

As we pass a bouncer, I say, "Tell Monica that Camille drove Marcus home, and not to worry."

Monica

June 3, 2017   *1:00 a.m.*

Inside the Champagne Room the older guy sits in the middle of the small ten by ten space fixated on my ass. I bounce up and down, inches away from his face. This is his third time requesting a lap dance each time the tip doubles. Each time I let him touch a little more, even though the signs plastered around the room clearly state *"Touching the Dancers Strictly Prohibited."*

Tonight, he hands me five crisp one hundred dollar bills. I slide the bills inside my bikini top. I turn and bend over, expertly bounce up and down and make my cheeks clap, allowing Dark Suit to see and smell my phatty. I turn to see the bulge fighting the material holding back his erection. I lick my cherry red lips and stare at his dick like it's a meal and I haven't eaten in days.

Dark Suit's eyes glisten. I slowly slide on his lap, sensuously unbuckling his belt, and removing his pants. Dark Suit never takes his eyes off of me.

"You never called me," he says. "I was hoping you would call. I...I want to help you. I can help you."

I cover his mouth with mine and kiss him eagerly as I grind his rock hard dick.

I ain't impressed by men paying for a fantasy because they're tired of their sweat-pants wearing, no sex having, bitching, and complaining wives.

I don't want to hear another man promise to take care of me. I'd heard that line all my life. I'd stupidly believed them, time and time again.

🎩🎩🎩

The first was Ice. Ice, aka Carlos Rodrigo Espinosa, was a baller from my barrio. Dominican, he ran the Upper East Side, up to about the 140s, east of Fifth Avenue, and over to the East and Harlem rivers.

Ice was ten years older than me, and would watch me walking to school every day with my brothers.

"What up, Mami?" He'd say with the most intense stare I'd ever seen. It was like no one else was in the world but me and him.

"Uh, that's because he is cold through and through," my best friend Esmeralda said. "That's why they call him Ice, remember?"

Ice was known around the barrio for being a cold-hearted killer. He sliced a kid's neck in front of his mother because she owed him money and was late paying it back. He tossed one of his boys in front of a train in the subway because he had stolen some product from him to try and start his own crew. And rumor had it, that he was responsible for the blood bath at Sal's last year.

He wiped out Tony Rizzo's entire crew during their turf meeting in the basement. Every one of them, shot point blank, execution style. Tony had his dick shoved in his mouth. They said, to send a message that if you try to creep up on Ice's territory you were basically fuckin' yourself.

Still, there was something about Ice that got me all excited. It was a pull I couldn't resist. Even though I knew better, that day in August when Ice stepped up to me, instead of running off, I turned and faced him, hand on hip, in high cut denim daisy dukes and a red tube top, my thick, black Puerto Rican curls all over my head.

"What up, Papi?"

Ice chuckled, looking me up and down. I knew he was impressed by the way he smiled. Ice never smiled.

"You, Mami. What's good?"

I looked him up and down like I was inspecting him. I reached back and pulled my hair up in a ponytail, essentially pushing my titties out for Ice to see. His bulging eyes told me that he did. I got a rush from watching him watching me. I tried hard not to grin, but failed. Getting that reaction made me feel powerful.

"Yeah, you the shot caller around here, right?" We met eyes.

Ice chuckled. "Yeah, that's right." He leaned back against the wall.

"Well then, I suppose that would be *you*, Papi?"

For the next two years (ninth and tenth grades) I became Carlos' girl. Everybody called him Ice, except me. I called him Rodrigo.

Nobody called him Carlos. He was named after his dad who left his mom when he was seven. Ice was the oldest of six brothers and sisters. Ice took care of his family by running for the OG Dominican, Rene Antonio Aquino, responsible for expanding the Dominican drug trade into New York.

Rene was a typical Dominican immigrant to New York City. He arrived as a teen-ager with his parents, learned English reasonably well and became a diehard Yankees fan. Although he never finished high school, he managed to buy a bodega named *Diana's* on Wilson Avenue in Bushwick, Brooklyn, and enjoyed a middle-class life complete with sports cars and a couple of rental houses in Queens.

At eight, Ice had his own corner. By twelve, he had three runners and four corners. By sixteen, he was a General. At eighteen, Rene got locked up on charges of racketeering, drug trafficking, conspiracy to commit kidnapping and conspiracy to commit murder.

Ice was feuding with Pepi for Rene's territory. Pepi was twenty-six, and Rene's cousin. But Rene had a soft spot for Ice, calling him a real G with heart. Pepi was known to have his boys handle most of his dirty work, but Ice was ruthless and known for handling his business himself.

Rene sent Ice and Pepi both two keys of heroin to move as a test to determine who would take his place while he did his ten-year bid. Pepi used his family name to take up most of the corners in the barrio. Ice hooked up with two of his Guido friends from PS 126 with territory along the Eastern Seaboard, doubling his take on the sales and spreading Rene's territory further north.

"This G not only got heart, this motherfucker got smarts!" Rene said, handing his territory over to Ice two days before he was taken into custody.

Twenty-four hours after Rene was locked up, Ice walked up on Pepi and shot him point blank in the chest. Pepi's crew became Ice's crew, and it stayed that way for four years, until Ice's General, Octavio turned state's evidence with the DEA for a plea bargain. For a reduced sentence, the deal included naming all the major players in the barrio.

Monica

For two years, I had been laced with the best of the best. I was devastated when my plush life as a dope dealer's girlfriend came to a screeching halt my second year of high school when Ice got locked up

I had always been an amazing dancer, dancing with my crew *The Boricuan Mafia* for years. We would battle other girl dance groups in the barrio and had gained a reputation for being the tightest crew in the Bronx. I choreographed most of our routines and Esmeralda would put on the finishing touches with her background in gymnastics.

My mom was relieved when Ice went to jail. To keep me from staying on that path she made me try out for Fiorello H. LaGuardia High School because it wasn't in the 'hood and "No estaba lleno de matone".

I don't know how she knew it wasn't full of hoodlums, but what I was sure Yolis didn't know was that I was hanging tough with *her* sister Gladys.

Tia Gladys is the opposite of her church going, family-oriented sister, Yolis. She is wild and all about making money. So when I ask my Tia how she stays stacked, my aunt smirks and says, "Hija, you gotta have a huge ass pair of cajones to make the kind of money your Tia makes."

I don't have any balls. But I have to find a way to make money to support myself. I think about how Ice got put on at such a young age.

"I got heart. What I got to do?

Tia Gladys looks me up and down. "What can you do, hija? And I mean, what can you that a nigga wanna pay you to do it?"

I think for a minute. Then I show her the latest routine I had just choreographed for a battle with the SoHo crew next week.

My moves are powerful: strong and sensual, but all about hip hop moves – poppin and flexin'.

When I finish my routine, Tia Gladys flicks her cigarette to the ground with a huge grin across her face.

"Got damn, Boricua! Yo ass is about to be paid."

I tell my mom I'm on a dance team at school. She is so happy that when I leave a couple of nights a week "to practice" or "go to a performance", it doesn't faze her. But I'm really hanging with my aunt, stripping for older men at bachelor parties.

They start off innocent enough, I do a sexy routine and strip down to what is the equivalent of a two-piece bikini. Because I'm so young, my body is tight: thick, muscular thighs, washboard abs, and a full plump ass that turns every head in the room.

Tia Gladys is my manager. She books the parties and negotiates the prices. I choose the music, choreograph the routines, and design my costumes.

Very early on, Tia Gladys tells me, "You gotta take all that hip hop shit out of your routines, hija. Move your pussy and ass more. Men want a fantasy, not some battle."

She gave me a few porn flicks to watch. "Look at what them ho's is selling. The fantasy: the hooker heels, the lingerie, the long lashes and hair. They all do the same shit, they fuck them. But it's the fantasy these men want. Half them Bitches ain't even wet. Look at their coochies. Dry as shit. But they moan and groan like those dicks is the best thing since pan de leche."

I watch the porn over and over. At first, all they do is get me horny. It's been months since I've had sex. Ice is locked up and I've been spending so much time with Tia Gladys that I haven't had time to hook up with anyone—not that anyone is even interested me. Ice is a man. All these new kids on the block are boys.

I become very familiar with my body; masturbating has shown me exactly where my spots are. Soon I'm masturbating every day without the porn. When I do my routines for the horny men I get turned on by their hard dicks and even let the cute ones suck on my breasts and slide their fingers inside my wet pussy. Tia Gladys never says a word.

"A little touching gets you more money, Boricua. Get that money, Bitch."

After our first year, Tia Gladys has a developed a reputation and can't keep up with all the requests.

"Boricua, don't you have no home girls you can get to cover some of these parties? We missing out on money," she says one night looking at all her requests. She flicks her cigarette and looks at me.

"You and me, we can clean up. You can run the girls, and I'll run the business."

I think for a minute. "And how much will you cut me in?"

Tia Gladys chuckles. "You know you my family, all about that dollar." She laughs. "I ain't mad at you, Boricua. You get me five Bitches; we charge a hundred and twenty dollars per girl. You get eighty, I get a hundred twenty, and the girls get seventy-five and whatever tips they make. The remaining twenty-five we'll use for marketing and advertising -- flyers and shit."

I think about how many parties I do a week, and how much money that will add up to with five girls doing the same—I will clean up.

"Deal!"

I pull in my girls from the Boricuan Mafia to work for her. For six months, Tia Gladys books bachelor parties. Then one night, Tia says to me, "Mija, we need to control our money."

"What are you talking about Tia? We are controlling our money."

"Are we?" she says, taking a deep drag on her cigarette. Her right eye is half-open, squinted closed from the cigarette smoke. The half smoked cigarette dangles from the right corner of her mouth. "We dance when niggas have bachelor parties."

I look at Tia like she's lost her mind. "Yes?"

"Yeah, we need to dance when we want to. Not when they need us to," Tia Gladys says "That way, we control the money."

I give her a blank stare.

"Boricua, if we held private parties and invited dudes to come to us we could have parties every weekend as opposed to two to three weekends a month, waiting on some schlep to get married," Tia explains.

I sit quietly taking in all Tia is saying. I quickly understand the dollars and sense of Tia's reasoning.

The next week we are hosting a naughty girl party in Tia Gladys's living room. It is twenty-five dollars to get in. The pay is the same for the girls, seventy-five dollars for the night and whatever tips they got. I get a few of my homeboys to be security, since it is Tia Gladys's house, we can't have no niggas acting stupid and thinking we couldn't shut it down. Gladys always packs heat, but with the homies, she won't have to pull her .38 special out to "have a quiet conversation" with nobody, as she puts it.

Two months in, Tia Gladys adds a bar. She serves beer, wine and a signature drink, usually vodka and cranberry juice or gin and juice. That racks up quite a bit of money. She tries serving food: hot dogs, chips—cheap and easy food, but after she finds mustard and ketchup stains on her carpet, she cuts that shit out.

After six months, me and Tia G are filling up the room.

"We need some more girls," Tia says scanning the room. "Maybe even some dudes."

I nod.

The next day, she's passing out flyers looking for new dancers. We hold auditions that following week from seven to nine p.m. anyone interested has to show up and do a two-minute routine. They are performing for me and Tia.

Some are cute but horrible performers. Some are ugly as shit, but have great stage presence. Tia G is good at her job.

"The crowd will eat her up. She's wet behind the ears, but you can teach her how to move," she says, watching a light-skinned girl with long straight hair and bangs bend over backwards, then flip her legs over and land into a split.

"His ass got good moves, he's just too ugly," Tia G says about one of the dudes from the hood. "Let's try him for a couple of sessions. If he can bring in some dollars, we'll keep him. If not, he's got to go. Let him know that when we take him on," Tia says.

I nod, jotting down notes on my notepad.

I know like Tia, all he is going to do is get women to show up and support him. Tia G doesn't care. If he pads every performance with women he knows, she doesn't care. We are going to get paid regardless.

Less than a year into the game we are making nothing less than twelve hundred a night. Tia is getting requests from regulars to spend time with her dancers. At our monthly meeting, Tia G announces that the following week they will be adding the Boom Boom Room.

"No one is required to do anything with anyone, *ever*," Tia G says, taking a long puff off the cigarette. "But, if you want to – there is money to be made. In the Boom Boom Room, you get to set your price and do as much as you want. If you say only oral – then the customer will agree to your terms or nothing happens.

"If you want to have sex, the set price for straight sex is one hundred dollars, half of that goes to the house. If you want more of the cut, then you raise your price and take the difference. It's up to you. If the client wants to fuck you bad enough, he'll pay. If not, no loss. But it's up to you to set your prices up front. There will be condoms in the room and a backroom exit to maintain privacy. And Dre will be outside to regulate any crazies asking you to do anything you don't want to do," Tia explains.

"But we don't have to, right?" Jasmine asks.

"Right. You don't have to anything you don't want to do," Tia G says.

The following week, Tia G discretely mentions the Boom Boom Room to a few of the regulars she knows who come to see the same girls over and over.

"Hey, Mike."

"What's up, Tia G?"

"Remember when you asked me if I could introduce you to Diamond?"

"Yeah. You said no nigga."

Tia G laughs.

"Yeah, well. My girls don't date customers." Tia G takes a long drag on her cigarette and stubs out the butt in the ashtray. "But, if you want to spend a little time with Diamond, I might be able to arrange it."

A huge smile stretches across Mike's face. "Is that right?"

"Yeah nigga, that's right. You interested?"

"Hell yeah, I'm interested. I think Diamond is beautiful."

"Beautiful enough for you to drop two hundred dollars for an hour?"

Mike didn't hesitate. "Hell yeah. I spend more than that on trees." He reaches down into his pocket and pulls out a wad of cash. He peels off two one hundred dollar bills and hands them to Tia G who slides the money into her right tittie.

"I got two rules. And if you break these rules, Dre will break your fuckin' face, you understand me?"

Mike nods.

"Rule one: my girls only do what they want to do. Discuss all that shit upfront. Don't get into the room and try and do some shit you never discussed. You do that shit and Dre will beat yo ass, then toss you out on yo ass, *and* you lose yo money. You understand me?"

"Yeah. That shit seems fair."

"It is, right?" Tia G says with a smirk. "Rule two: discretion. I ain't running no brothel. I'm just trying to keep my customers happy. You see what I'm sayin'? If you wanna get down in the Boom Boom Room, you two consenting adults, that shit ain't my business. But don't come up to me all loud and shit. We gone come up with some signal or some place you stand when you first come, to see if yo girl wanna get down that night."

"Yeah. Yeah," Mike says.

"The Boom Boom Room is in the back of the house, off to the side. When you leave, you exit the back door. Don't come back in through the house. You understand?"

"Yeah. I got you." Mike shifts. "Can I go see Diamond now?"

That first night, she made an additional seven hundred and fifty dollars.

Peaches has an admirer who's been following her for quite some time. After Peaches' performance he walks up to Tia G and says, "I'd like to spend some time with Peaches, please."

"Well, now, that depends on Peaches and if she wants to spend time with you," Tia G says.

Tia asks Peaches if she wants to get down.

"Shit, I need three hundred dollars to pay for my new weave." She looks out at the guy standing in the corner waiting for Tia G. "Yeah, I'll fuck that nigga," Peaches says. "Tell him anal is a extra fifty, though."

Tia G nods and said she will run the cost by the client.

"Peaches said she don't mind spending some time with you."

The man smiles broadly.

"It's going to cost you three hundred for one hour. Anal is a extra fifty dollars," Tia G says.

"That's fine." He reaches for his wallet. "I'll pay the extra fifty, too."

And right there, the Boom Boom Room takes off.

Clients are packing Tia G's living room and there are lines waiting to get in the Boom Boom Room.

I am cleaning up. I'm still performing, and occasionally taking a customer or two in the Boom Boom Room myself if I have something I really want to buy. After about twelve months I'm almost bringing in as much as I did when Ice used to kick me down.

A few customers ask me if they can take care of me. They want me to stop dancing and be with them. I smile and kiss them and look into their eyes. "You are so sweet. But you don't make enough to take care of me. I have very expensive taste."

And of course after that, they profess their undying love and tell me all that they will do for me.

It usually results in very expensive gifts for a couple of months—gifts I gladly accept, but it never goes further than that. Most of them are married men wanting a side Bitch, and I'm never going to be nobody's side Bitch.

Me and Tia G are looking to move the business out of the house to a commercial building. It has gotten so packed we move to two shows a night, one at nine and one at eleven. The money is good and I'm stacking most of it to pay for Law School when the unthinkable happens: Tia G dies.

Dre finds her laid out in her kitchen. She has a heart attack. It's the summer before I'm to start eleventh grade.

I do a couple of bachelor parties here and there, but I never try to revitalize the business.

Monica

June 3, 2017   *2:05 a.m.*

When I hook up with Marcus I try to act like a normal girlfriend and let go of the club dancing. But when he gets tagged the end of our freshman year in college, I audition for Sin & Seduction Gentlemen's Club in the Bronx. He does two years for giving a friend a ride who had committed armed robbery, and I do what I have to do in order to pay for college.

When I start, the dancers are old, their routines stale. I have no problem coming up with a routine that has the manager salivating. And I keep the house packed the nights I'm performing. I come up with the stage name X'Stacy, and start back stacking my chips for law school, my ticket to financial freedom and complete independence.

Yeah, I'm older and wiser now. All a man can do for me at this point is give me what I can't give myself . . . money. Once I graduate from law school I'll make my own money and take care of myself. But for now, for always, I fuck with men on my own terms.

CHAPTER EIGHT

The Reunion

"I'm afraid that some times
You'll play lonely games too.
Games you can't win
'cause you'll play against you." [10]

Camille

June 3, 2017   *1:30 a.m.*

Marcus and I almost topple over twice trying to make it up the stairs to his apartment. His arm is around my neck and mine is around his waist.

"Marcus, I need you to try and walk up the stairs, you're heavy."

"Okay, Cam," he says, but he continues to hang on my shoulder.

It takes us a good half hour to navigate two flights of stairs, but we finally make it.

Once inside, Marcus stumbles across the room to his closet where he puts his Glock away. He walks over to the Bose sound system and turns on a booty shaking song. He turns the volume up high.

"Why don't you shake yo ass for me? I bet you move way better than yo girl. The quiet ones always do," Marcus says.

I walk over to the stereo, reach around Marcus and turn the volume down.

"Stop trippin', you're drunk."

---

[10] Dr. Seuss, *"Oh, The Places You'll Go!"* verse 26

Marcus yanks my hand away from the stereo and turns it up even louder. I grab my tote bag and walk toward the door. Marcus lunges in front of me. Blocking me with his body, he reaches back and slams the door.

I turn my back to him and smile, then place my hands on my hips and sigh deeply to let him know how exasperated I am. I turn slowly to face him. He's grinning at me, but I roll my eyes in feigned disgust in return, and walk past him.

As I do, he grabs my arm causing the contents of my bag to go flying all over his studio apartment.

"Marcus! Look at what you've done." I bend down and start to pick up my stuff off his floor. He's watching me down on all fours, crawling across his floor and his grin widens.

"Yo, Cam. Why you come here tonight?'

I sit up on my knees and look at him.

"Because yo ass was drunk and about to get your head blown off by that bouncer, remember?"

"Shit. That nigga know better. He knows who the fuck I am."

"Is that right? Because from where I was sitting, not only did he *not* know, but he didn't give a damn."

Marcus sucks his teeth. "Shit. That nigga know!" He grabs a wood bat out the corner of the room and walks around bangin' it on the floor. "And if he don't know, he about to know in a minute."

"Why will he know in a minute?"

Marcus pauses. I can tell he's contemplating his next words. He spins on his heels. He bangs his bat on the floor after every word. "Because I'm about to blow the fuck up! The Williams legacy returns!" Marcus stumbles as he lifts the bat over his head. "Tonight as a matter of fact."

I turn to face him. "What's happening tonight?" Nothing I could tell, based on how drunk he was.

"Tonight, I become a shot caller, baby," Marcus says. "Yeah, you should be trying to get wit me because I'm about to blow up."

I continue to pick up the rest of my stuff off his floor.

"Check this out. I got this dirty cop who was supposed to turn in two keys of cocaine on a bust he did. But instead he gave it to me to flip in my brothers' old neighborhood."

My eyes widen. "You're selling drugs, Marcus?"

"I'm about to blow up. This cop is going to be my source. He's going to get me this stolen shit, and I'ma turn that shit over and make bank. And, because it's his shit, I won't have to worry about 5-0. So I'm about to blow the fuck up. Hey! You remember T? The one who got me the kicks back in the day?"

I smile, remembering those good times with him. "Yeah, I remember him."

"Yeah, he's the one I'ma hook up with later tonight to move the powder." Marcus points the bat toward a duffle bag in the corner of the room. "You can't just have anybody move that much shit. It's got to be somebody you can trust."

I turn to find Marcus smiling broadly. I remember that smile. I remember his fingers, his tongue, all the exploring we did as horny teenagers in high school.

I search his face and wonder if he ever felt bad about how he did me? He knew I loved him. He used to love me, too. But when Monica came on the scene it changed everything for us.

He left me. So that he could have sex with Monica.

🎩 🎩 🎩

Marcus is looking at me. I still look the same for the most part.

I wonder if he's remembering, if he misses me, us. There is something in his face. Something beneath that hard exterior that I still recognize.

I know Marcus' innocence is gone. Even after he and Monica got together he still had his boyish ways. But jail changed all of that.

I'd heard how jail could make brothers hard. The things they endured. How it made them feel afterward: always questioning themselves, like they always had to prove to themselves *and more importantly, to others,* that they were real men.

I don't know what all Marcus went through those two years in jail, but I know he came out different. He came out mean and hard. But for a split second, I thought I saw my old Marcus.

Marcus snaps. He pulls me up off the floor and into his chest. He shoves his tongue deep into my mouth.

I open my mouth to receive him, moaning. He slides his hand up my skirt and into my panties, finding my clit with ease. It was like we were back in high school again, he knew exactly where to touch me.

"Oh," I whimper. "Marcus . . ." Marcus walks me to his bed.

I lay back and he removes my panties. He spreads my thighs apart and gently starts to lick me. I lift my butt and grab his head. "Yes. Oh, yes. It feels . . it feels so good."

Marcus slides his finger inside me while he sucks on my clit. I moan as I watch him expertly bring me to a climax. Marcus looks up and smiles.

"Damn you taste good, girl."

My heart is beating so loud, all I can hear is swooshing in my head.

He stands and unbuckles his belt. He drops his pants and draws and frees the super hard wood.

I watch. Remembering. When I see his super hard dick, I can't help but spread my legs wide. I can't wait to feel him inside me.

"Yeah, I know you want this dick. You've wanted it since you were a homey little freshman."

"You gonna do that to Monica?" I coo.

Marcus laughs. "She did it to you."

I frown. But before I can reply, Marcus unfastens my bra and takes my breast in his mouth and sucks it greedily. I toss my head back and grab the back of his head. He lays sloppy kisses on my chest and neck then covers my mouth with his.

I lift my hips - Marcus tries to enter me.

"Mmm." I bite my bottom lip.

"Damn." He tries again. This time he gets further in. I take a deep breath as he pushes even farther in. It's uncomfortable the first few strokes, but after that, he feels so good inside me.

"Oh, yes!" I moan.

I didn't know anything could feel better than Marcus' tongue. But feeling him deep inside me filled me with such warmth and completeness.

"Fuck, your pussy is wet," Marcus says. "And tight. Got damn. Yo shit feels like virgin pussy."

"Because it is," I whisper in his ear.

"What? You stayed a virgin all these years?" I feel his dick harden inside me.

"All these years," I moan.

Looking into my eyes, he kisses me. I eagerly take his tongue into my mouth.

"You been waiting to give this tight ass pussy to me, baby?"

"Yes. I miss you. I love you, Marcus. I never stopped."

Marcus looks shocked. "Is that right?"

"Yes. I love you and I know you love me, too. Monica . . . Monica can't love you the way I love you."

A sinister look covers Marcus' face. He pulls out, and flips me over on my stomach. He pulls my hips back toward him and tries to penetrate me anally.

"What the fuck are you doing?" I scream.

"Show me how much you love me, Cam." He tries to enter me from behind.

"Marcus, no." I struggle to get from underneath him. "I'm giving myself to you. That's not enough?"

"Your pussy is good and tight. Your ass has got to be even tighter. Come on, if you love me. Show me." He tries to pin me down.

My heart is pounding inside my head. "Marcus! Stop!"

"What, Bitch? Now you too good?" Marcus screams.

"To be fucked in the ass? Hell yeah," I say, trying to squirm from underneath him.

He's strong, and pulls me up on all fours. I struggle with him, and try to elbow him in his side so I can get away.

Marcus picks me up, flips me back over and slaps me in the face. The force sends me flying to the floor.

"Fuck you then, you ugly Bitch! I didn't want to fuck yo ugly ass anyway!" Marcus screams. "I just felt sorry for you."

On my way down to the floor, I slam my cheek on the corner of the footboard.

Marcus pulls up his pants, fastens his belt and walks toward the bathroom mumbling, "Worthless Bitches . . . think they too good . . . don't nobody want you."

I slowly pull myself up and sit on the floor, naked, embarrassed and now I'm getting pissed.

Marcus glares at me and laughs as he staggers into the bathroom.

I can't believe this. I'm mortified. All these years, I waited to give myself to him. And this is how he treats me?

I can feel the anger start to well up inside me . . . it feels like hot lava bubbling up inside. Rising. About to explode . . .

In a panic, I frantically reach for my tote bag and search for my cell phone. I find it and quickly dial Jacky.

CHAPTER NINE

Girls' Weekend!

"And you may not find any
you'll want to go down.
In that case, of course,
you'll head straight out of town." [11]

Jacqueline

June 3, 2017   *2:17 a.m.*

Monica and I walk out of the club laughing and talking. My trap phone rings from inside my Coach bag. It's after 2:00 a.m. *Who the hell is calling me at this hour?* I pull it out, flip open the case, and read my caller ID.

"It's Cam," I say looking confused.

"Why is she calling on your trap phone?" Monica says.

I'm wondering the same thing.

"Hello?" I say. "Cam? What's wrong? What's going on?" I turn to Monica and mouth, 'She's crying.'

"Cam, slow down. I can't understand a word you're saying." I close my eyes to try and concentrate. She repeats what she said. My eyes pop open.

"Where are you?" I pause as she tells me. "Don't move. We're on our way!"

"What's going on?" Monica says.

---

[11] Dr. Seuss, *"Oh, The Places You'll Go!"* verse 4

"I don't know . . . something with Marcus." I throw my phone into my purse and frantically search for my keys. Monica and I rush to my car.

I pull up to Marcus' apartment. Monica hops out at the curb, and darts up the stairs two at a time. There's no parking.

I circle the block looking for a space. Everybody's in for the night so finding a park is going to be impossible. And double parking is out of the question. I make a right on Birchall Ave., speed down the block and make another right on Bronx River Parkway, punching it back to Sagamore Street. I see break lights ahead as I turn the corner.

A red Vega is leaving just as I approach Marcus' apartment.

I pull in, throw the car in park and jump out. I run as fast as I can toward Marcus' building, as I approach I see Camille standing outside the front door holding a green trash bag. I grab her. Her blouse is ripped, her face is streaked with tears and she has a bruised cheek.

"Cam, what's going on?"

She is unresponsive. I grab the bag and open it.

"Oh my God, Cam, what happened?" I scream. I walk her down to my car.

Monica

June 3, 2017   *3:27 a.m.*

I splash my face with cold water. I toss my head back, grab my hair and tie it up in a bun on the top of my head.

Standing in front of the sink, I stare into the mirror. I blink several times, trying to focus. My eyes are fixed on the image over my right shoulder.

Yep, it's my boyfriend's lifeless body sprawled across cold tile in the middle of his bathroom floor.

Dark red blood encircles his head.

Jacqueline

June 3, 2017   *3:57 a.m.*

"What the fuck?" I scream as I open the trunk and toss the trash bag in it. Then I pace back and forth. "What the fuck happened, Camille?"

Camille is leaning on my car, clutching her tote handbag, rocking back and forth, rubbing a charm on her necklace, staring into space.

Monica backs out the door, arms full of Marcus' things. "Grab some of this shit!'

I run and grab a DVD player, X-Box, a Bose SoundTouch system, and Beats by Dr. Dre headphones. Monica runs back inside and picks up the trail of items down the hall that fell out of her arms.

"What is this?" I say.

"Marcus' most expensive shit," Monica says, looking around. Seeing no one, she tosses it in the back seat of my car. "Let's fucking go!"

I grab Camille's arm, but she yanks it away.

"Marcus is dead!" Camille says. "We have to call the police."

I turn to face Monica. Monica runs around the car to where Camille and I are standing.

"That's the last fucking thing we're going to do." She grabs Camille's right arm and I grab the left and we lead her to the car.

"But, he's dead." Camille turns to face Monica. "Your boyfriend is dead." Tears stream down her face.

Monica pulls her into her arms. "Marcus attacked you." Monica rubs Camille's back. "He was a mean son of a Bitch. He's not the person you were in love with back in high school, Cam. He went to jail and came back angry and abusive." Monica pulls back and looks at Camille. The bruise was becoming more prominent and her left eye was swollen.

"He hit the wrong Bitch," I say and shove Camille's head down into the back of my car like I worked for the NYPD. I slide behind the wheel and Monica jumps into the passenger's seat. We speed off into the darkness, minds reeling, trying to process everything that just took place, and what the hell we were going to do next.

Camille

June 3, 2017   *4:17 a.m.*

As we speed off into the night, I can't help but replay Monica's words 'he's not the person you were in love with back in high school. He went to jail and came back angry and abusive.'

It was true. But if he had been with me, he never would have traveled down that path.

> *You can get so confused that you'll start in to race*
> *down long wiggled roads at a break-necking pace*
> *and grind on for miles cross weirdish wild space,*
> *headed, I fear, toward a most useless place.*
> *The Waiting Place...*[12]

---

[12] Dr. Seuss, *'Oh, The Places You'll Go!'* verse 18

This section of my favorite book by Dr. Seuss pops in my head. I'd ask my dad to read it to me over and over.

"Cam, don't you want daddy to read you another book?" he'd say pointing to all the other books on my bookshelf. But I never wanted him to. I loved this book. I loved the way he read it. I loved the rhythm of the rhymes, the pace of the words.

I had given Jacky and Monica special deluxe editions for their graduation. I had to explain to Monica the premise behind the book, and why I'd given it to them—she looked at me like I'd given her a bag of rocks.

It was obvious that reading wasn't a priority in her home.

I believe Marcus is in *The Waiting Place*. Or hell. I don't know for sure. I had prayed for his soul. Prayed for God's mercy. His spirit was free from this world. I hope it was resting with God up in heaven.

This time, the tears that flow are genuine.

I find myself crying for Marcus. Thinking about what he must have gone through to turn him into such a monster.

Jacqueline

June 3, 2017   4:17 a.m.

We drive in silence for about ten minutes.

"Slow down," Monica instructs. She rolls down the window and sticks her head out. "There! Pull up to that dumpster."

I pull over. Monica grabs a few of Marcus' things and jumps out. She looks around, then opens the dumpster lid and tosses in the stuff. We do this for two or three miles, reading posted signs that indicate trash day is on Monday.

"The trunk, Moni," I remind her on the last stop.

"There," Monica says slamming the trunk closed. She'd gotten rid of all the stuff, including the green trash bag. "They'll think it was a drug deal gone bad."

I nod. "That's plausible."

"We should call the police, guys. Just tell them it . . . it was self-defense," Camille mumbles.

"No!" Monica and I scream.

"If we did that now, we're accessories after the fact," Monica says. "And I'm not going to jail for anyone. Especially not Marcus Williams."

"That's right," I say. "Monica said she wiped down the apartment so there shouldn't be any traces of you. It will look too suspicious now if we say it was self-defense. There's no evidence, and whatever evidence was there has been destroyed. Nah, that's not a good equation for a sistah and the penal code system."

"But can't we just tell them I was scared . . . and you were trying to help me?"

"No!" Once again, Monica and I scream together.

Monica slides open her phone and starts texting.

"What are you doing?" I say.

She finishes her text and hits send. "I sent Marcus a text," She says. "It says 'Hey, don't forget, rollin' out with Jac and Cam this weekend to Vegas for Girls' Weekend. They're picking me up from the club tonight. See you Sunday! Xo'. That way it distances us from the apartment." Monica rubs her temples.

"Great idea." I nod "Bitch, you're going to make a fabulous lawyer one day." I grip the steering wheel extra hard.

Camille stares out the window.

We arrive at my place and pile out the car. In the elevator, I pull Camille close.

"It's going to be okay, Cam. I promise," I say in a whisper.

"How do you know?" Camille replies.

"Because we're your girls. We got your back."

Inside my apartment, I move quickly. I point Monica toward the fridge. She grabs a towel and fills it with ice. She places it over Camille's eye.

"Hey Cedric, what up daddy? It's JayRo," I say, grabbing a leather Michael Kors travel bag out of my closet.

I snap my fingers at Monica and point to my closet, then at the two of them. Monica starts grabbing clothes from the closet and tossing them on the bed.

Camille sits clutching her oversized tote, rocking, holding the ice to her eye.

"Yeah, me and my girls are thinking about heading your way for a girls weekend. Yeah, we just graduated from college and want to celebrate – Vegas style."

Monica stops and looks at me. I wink.

"Yes, that's exactly why I'm calling." I walk into the bathroom and return with toiletries and toss them in the bag. I grab a pen and piece of paper off my desk.

"Yeah. Okay. Got it. Under what name? Uh huh. And my girls? Okay. Got it. Yes, of course. Cuz there's always money to be made, son!" I laugh. "Yep. Yep. The Ritz Carlton. Yep. Got it. Uh huh. I got it, Cedric. Okay. I'll hit you up when we land. 'k. 'k. 'k. Oh okay, nigga, damn. This ain't my first time at the rodeo." I roll my eyes and flail my hands around. "Okay, good bye!" I swipe my phone closed.

I turn to my girls with a huge grin on my face.

"Buck up, ladies! We're headed out of town to celebrate our graduation!"

Monica turns to me and says, "What?"

Camille is still sitting and rocking, now biting her nails.

I start going through the outfits Monica picked out, separating them in three piles. I walk back into my closet and pick out a few more outfits for all of us.

"It's perfect! Just like you said, we will have alibis." I stop and place my hands on my hips. "Cedric has someone in ticketing at Southwest. She back-booked our flights to look like we planned this weeks ago. We have three tickets waiting for us at LaGuardia.

I grab my phone and walk over to where Camille is sitting and rocking.

"Come, Moni," I say, sliding in next to Camille. Monica slides in on the opposite side of Camille. I extend my right arm, holding my cell at a forty-five degree angle. "Smile, Bitches!"

I post the pic on FB, with the caption: *Proud graduates on our way to Sin City. What happens in Vegas, stays in Vegas! #TurnDown4What?*

CHAPTER TEN

Sin City

"You will come to a place where the streets are not marked.
Some windows are lighted. But mostly they're darked.
A place you could sprain both your elbow and chin!
Do you dare to stay out? Do you dare to go in?
How much can you lose? How much can you win?" [13]

Jacqueline

June 3, 2017   *12:30 p.m.*

"Hello Ms. Roberts," the lady behind the ticket counter says to me. "Welcome to Southwest Airlines."

"Thank you." I smile and turn to check on Camille and Monica.

Camille is clutching that damned purse, rocking like a re-re. I casually scan the area for any signs of the police. Nothing.

If we can get to Vegas and get some distance between us and that dead body. *OMG, I can't believe Marcus is dead.*

"There you go," the lady says, handing me a stack of envelopes. "Three round-trip tickets to Las Vegas, Nevada: Here's yours, Ms. Lopez's, and Ms. Coleman's."

I smile and quickly glance at her nametag. "Thank you, Mrs. Claiborne."

"My pleasure. Is there anything else I can do for you today?"

I shake my head, looking over my shoulder at Camille. I know she's in shock. She's loved Marcus for forever. I make my way back to where

---

[13] Dr. Seuss, *"Oh, The Places You'll Go!"* verse 16

they are sitting. Monica is posted next to Camille, standing guard. Although she's been Marcus' girl the past six years, I'm less concerned about her. She's lived a rough life that includes seeing death up close on more than one occasion. Not to mention, since Marcus' release from jail when he turned into a mean son-of-a-bitch.

"Whatever happened to him in there turned him into a different person. He used to be a sweet, loving young man. He was street smart and had his brothers' rep to give him street cred in his borough, but all his sweetness left him after that stint in the penitentiary."

"Okay, ladies!" I say, smiling broadly, holding up the tickets. "Next stop, Sin City! Let's put some distance between us and the Big Apple. I think we take advantage of this opportunity and make it a Girls' Graduation Weekend."

Monica forces a crooked smile. Camille continues to rock back and forth.

"Hey Ced, it's JayRo. We're here," I say as we pull into the parking lot. "Yep. Got it." I slide my phone close; grab my bag from the taxi and head through the double doors, Camille and Monica in tow.

"Good afternoon, welcome to the Ritz Carlton!" the attendant says as we make our way to the front desk.

"Good afternoon," Monica replies.

"Hello," I say, handing the young man behind the desk my credit card and I.D.

"Good afternoon, Ms. Anderson," he says, looking at the fake I.D. I always use when I'm running a scam "Checking in?"

"Yes, please," I reply.

"Great." He clicks on his keyboard. "I see we have you and two other adults in the penthouse? Ms. Devareaux and Ms. Spencer."

I smile and nod. He smiles and hands me my receipt and three keys.

"Oh my god, Jacqueline!" Monica screams as we enter the luxurious penthouse. "This shit is fucking fabulous!" She runs through every room in the suite, screaming and shouting, "Fucking look at this – two toilets! What the fuck do you need two toilets in the bathroom for?"

"It's a bidet, Bitch," I scream back, laughing.

Camille slumps down on the sofa in the seating area of the suite.

"This is the most amazing hotel I've ever seen," Monica says returning to the room.

"Only the best for my girls." I wink.

"How can you afford this?"

I hold up a credit card. "How can Vivian Greenwood afford this, you mean?" Both Camille and Monica's eyes widen. "And while we're here, you are Estelle Preston." I point to Camille. "And you're Gwendolyn McIntyre," I say pointing to Monica.

"Gwendolyn?" Monica says, but before she can go into full distress, my cell rings. I look at the caller I.D.

"It's Cedric!" I say, holding my hand up at Monica. I swipe my phone. "Hey Ced. Yes, we're in the penthouse now. Yes, it's gorgeous. We love it. Thank you." I walk toward my Michael Kors travel bag and start pulling out clothes.

"Yeah, okay. The Mirage? Uhn huh. Okay. Yep. Got it." I pull a cute little dress up to my chest and step in front of a full-length mirror. "Yes. Okay, like last time? Yes, I got it. And where will we meet up? Uh huh, okay. No problem!"

I turn to face the girls. "Okay, so here's the deal . . . we're going to go to the Mirage and have some fun!"

"Girls' Graduation Weekend!" Monica screams, pulling Camille up on to her feet.

I take a photo of them in front of the Ritz logo on the wall. I Snap Chat it with the caption that reads: *Off to Vegas, Bitches!*

CHAPTER ELEVEN

Giving Chase

"You can get so confused
That you'll start in to race
Down long wiggled roads at a break-necking pace
And grind on for miles cross weirdish wild space." [14]

Detective Morales

June 3, 2017   *2:30 p.m.*

"Sir," a rookie cop says to me as I enter the crime scene, "the victim is Marcus Williams. Twenty-three year old African American male."

I cough uncontrollably. I put my hand up and walk out into the hallway to catch my breath and to compose myself after hearing who this vic is.

The rookie follows behind me as I walk toward the stairs. "Signs around the room indicate burglary." I nod, suddenly anxious about the situation. *Did they steal the stolen evidence? Did they know about me?*

I clear my throat, turn, and walk into Marcus' tiny apartment. I'd never been here before. All of our meetings took place in Midtown.

I scan the room looking for any signs of my shit.

The problem with this situation was that this didn't just involve me. I had over a dozen other people involved. Two cops in the evidence room who made sure only half the drugs confiscated get recorded. There was Scerillo and Johnston who moved it to a safe

---

[14] Dr. Seuss, *'Oh, The Places You'll Go!'* verse 18

house. Donatelli and Washington who received it at the safe house. and of course, there were four detectives on the gang squad who made the busts and stole the evidence. It was our supplemental pension plan. And damned if I'm the reason this shit blows up in our faces. Some of these cats have been on the force for over 40 years. If this came out, they'd be branded dirty cops and tossed out on their asses without a second thought. Pensions gone, just like that!

"Cause of death appears to be a blunt force to the head."

I stand in the center of the room and slowly take it all in. *I can't believe this shit. This muthafucka up and gets killed before he flips my shit.*" I run my fingers through my hair.

"Thank you, Officer Quinn." He hesitates and then leaves the room.

I feel for loose panels inside the closet and the walls around the room. I get on all fours and check the slats on the floor. *Nothing.* I pause, lowering my head, and as I look to the right, I catch a glimpse of something under the bed.

I reach for it. It's a business card. It's blue on one side, with handwriting on the back. *"603 West 45th.* The card belongs to Robert Hagerman. Vice President, Acquisitions. National Accounts. Paraco Gas Corporation, New Hyde Park, New York.

I slide the card into my jacket and finish checking the area for the stolen cocaine, money, or evidence of a transaction. Nothing.

"Detective Morales, sir?" The rookie enters the room carrying a bloody bat.

I stand. "The murder weapon?"

"Yes sir. We believe so."

I nod. "Be sure to get it to CSI right away," I say. "Where did you find it?"

"Someone threw it down the hopper."

"Now why would someone toss the murder weapon down a trash chute instead of taking it with them?" I take the plastic covered metal bat from the cop, eyeing it up and down.

"Maybe they thought it would be destroyed in the trash compactor?"

I hand him back the bat and shake my head. "No. Doesn't make sense. Maybe back in the day when the trash chutes led to a basement incinerator, where it would be burned." I walk out the apartment and into the hallway with the officer following behind me. I pull open the chute and look down.

"Incinerators were banned in most New York City residential buildings in the 1980s," the officer said. "Today, building refuse is routed to trash compactors where it's squashed and picked up by the sanitation department or a private carting company."

I turn and face the rookie. "Well, I guess the perp is either a dumb criminal or didn't think this crime all the way through."

"I guess so," I reply and head for the stairs. Before I'm out the door, I'm dialing Robert Hagerman.

"Hello Detective," Robert Hagerman says as I enter his office. "How may I help you?"

"I'm investigating a homicide."

The gentleman's head snaps back. His blue eyes bulge. He quickly throws his hands up. "Whoa! I don't have anything to do with a homicide!" he says, quickly glancing outside his office door and shutting it. "Why, why would you think I have anything to do with a murder?"

I watch him walk behind his desk, sit, and stare up at me. Furrowed brows create a deep crease in the center of his forehead.

I hand him the blue business card. "Is this yours?"

"Yes . . . it . . . it is." His face quickly moves from shock to fear as he flips the card over. I can see he knows the address on the back of the card by the way he stares at it.

"We found it at the crime scene," I say, watching him closely. "Do you know Marcus Williams?"

"Who? No. I don't. I'm sorry."

"He lives in a three story apartment building in the Bronx, off Unionport and Sagamore Street."

"I don't know why it was there, Detective. I don't know anyone in the Bronx. No one on Unionport and Sagamore Streets," he says as he studies the handwriting on the back of the card.

"Do you recognize the address, or the handwriting, sir?"

Mr. Hagerman pauses.

"Listen, if you have nothing to do with this case, the best thing you can do is clear your name. I'm not here to start any trouble." I look out the huge clear paned window. "Once I have the information I need, I'm done here. But until I get a lead on who killed this young man, I will have to keep following up on every piece of evidence that I have. And quite honestly, you're all I've got right now. So, if you know something, now would be a good time to share it."

"Yes. I recognize the address and handwriting," he says, without looking up. "The address is Sin and Seduction. It's a . . . Gentleman's club in Midtown." He looks up at me. "I gave my card to a dancer there the other night." He blushes.

"I know the place. On the corner of Eleventh and West?" I scribble the name of the club on my notepad.

"Yes. That's the place."

"And what's the dancer's name?"

"X'stacy," he says, eyes down. "She's a really nice girl, Detective Morales. Not like the other girls there. She's smart, you know? Really smart." He looks up at me and we lock eyes.

I nod and smile. Knowing he's a sucker being played, but not caring. *Hey, if he liked it, I loved it.* I've never been in a position where I had to pay for pussy. But the reality is, men always end up paying for it one way or another. In my opinion, men like Hagerman might be the smart ones – get what you want without all the drama that comes with a relationship.

"I gave her my card and told her to call me if she ever needed anything."

"Did she call you? Did she need you to take care of Marcus?"

"No!" he replies before I can finish the sentence. "I mean, she's asked for things before . . . help with her LSAT fees." He looks up at me. "She's really smart. I'm telling you, she's different."

"What's X'Stacy's real name?"

"I . . . I don't know. She wouldn't tell me," he says, but quickly follows up with, "She's been burnt by other men. They've stalked her. I told her it was fine. I wanted her to learn to trust me. That takes time."

I nod, giving the appearance—I hope—that I believed every word he was telling me. "Of course. Has she ever called you before?"

"No. Never. And she's never asked me for anything directly. We go into the uh, back room, and she tells me what she's up to." He smiles sheepishly. "I give her, you know, *big tips*," he says using air quotes. "To help her out, like for the test fees."

I nod my head.

"But she's there four nights a week. Thursday, Friday, and Saturdays, and every other Tuesday. She used to dance on Wednesdays, but she has classes on Wednesday nights now."

I stand. Mr. Hagerman stands. I extend my hand and he shakes it.

"Thank you, sir," I say and head to the door. "I appreciate your help." I hand him my card. "If you remember anything else you think might be important, please don't hesitate to call."

He nods and opens his door. "I do hope everything is okay with Stacy."

I pause for a half second, make the connection with the name, then nod and smile.

"Thank you for your time and assistance today."

I pull up to the strip club I was just at three nights ago. I didn't realize the night I followed Marcus would be the last time I'd see his punk ass alive.

I flash my badge at the bouncer who steps back and lets me in.

Inside the dank room are girls swinging on poles. One is upside down with her legs spread wide open. Another is spinning around, again, legs spread eagle. And on the center stage is an old broad with blonde Beyoncé looking hair, twerking while men stuff dollar bills in her sparkly gold G-string. It's hot and musty in the smoke-filled room.

"I'm looking for X'Stacy," I say to the big bald bartender.

"You and every nigga in this place," he replies stone-faced.

I flash my badge.

His face doesn't change. "What business you got with her?" he grunts.

"Homicide investigation," I say. No response. "Marcus Williams was found dead in his apartment this morning."

The bartender stops mixing the drink and looks me in the eyes. "Not surprised. He was a Bitch, was only a matter of time before somebody clipped his ass."

"Is that right?" I say, sliding on to a stool. "And why is that?"

He returned to mixing his drink. "Because Marcus Williams was a two bit hustler trying to live up to his brothers' reputation." He placed the drink on the counter for the waitress. "But he didn't have the heart or the balls to play on that court."

I didn't like hearing that shit. Marcus talked a good game. Had me thinking he *was* on the same level as his brothers, only he was smarter because he was educated. He said he played a smarter game. Where his brothers were ruthless, he was strategic. He had me believing his bullshit.

"So where is X'Stacy?" I say, scanning the room.

"She ain't here."

"Was she here last night?"

"Yes."

"How long?"

"All night."

"'Til what time?"

"'Til her set was done. Around two a.m."

I jot down notes. The coroner puts Marcus' murder between one and three a.m.

"She didn't kill him." He shakes his head. "She loved that piece of shit. He sent her in here black and blue most nights. I offered to break his scrawny little neck, but she wouldn't let me. She would always make excuses for his sorry ass."

"Well maybe you got tired of seeing her walk in black and blue. Maybe you decided to break his scrawny little neck as a favor. You seem quite fond of – what's X'Stacy's real name?"

The bartender smirks. "Yeah, that's why I told you that. So I could move to the top of your suspect list." He pauses and chuckles. "That cat ain't worth my livelihood. He got what he deserved. I knew it would come." He places another drink on the counter. "Her name is Monica Lopez. And she's a good kid. She's not like these other women up in here. She's a smart girl. She's got her head on straight. She punks a couple of Johns here and there, but she's in school. She ain't gone fuck up her plans over no trick like Marcus, trust me."

I spin around on the stool and take in all that the bartender and Hagerman said about this girl. If she was so smart, then why was she with Marcus, especially if he was beating her ass the way he's saying he did.

"Did Marcus come into the club last night?" I say, watching a woman with fuchsia pink hair drop it, and clap cheeks that would give J-Lo a run for her money. They were literally clapping – like two hands clapping!

"Yeah, his ass is in here every night Monica dances. Getting fucked up because his insecure ass can't stand seeing men gawking over his girl. Stupid. It's the dumbest shit you could ever witness."

"What time did he leave?"

"I don't know, I wasn't watching a clock. His drunk ass stumbled out before Monica took the stage, though. She goes on between one and one fifteen. Just depends on the girl ahead of her."

I hand him my card. "Did he leave by himself?" He reads the card.

"Detective Morales," he says. "I don't know. When he's at the bar, he's usually flirting with whoever has a slit between her legs. So I'm not really paying him no mind, if you understand what I'm trying to tell you about this loser." He finally stops and places all of his attention on me.

"I do. What about Monica? Did she leave by herself last night?"

"No. She left with a girlfriend. I know because I usually walk her out."

"Do you recall the girlfriend's name?"

He just stares at me.

"Thank you for your time. If you remember anything else about last night that you think would help the investigation, please give me a call."

At the station, I put in a request for copies of Marcus' telephone records. In the meantime, I pull the criminal record of Monica Lopez and come up empty.

"Detective Morales?" an intern interrupts my thoughts. "The phone records for the Williams case, sir."

"Thank you, David." I take the file and flip through the pages. Last text was from Monica's cell. *Bingo!*

I grab my jacket and head for the door. Sin City, here I come!

CHAPTER TWELVE

Crapped Out

"And IF you go in, should you turn left or right...
or right-and-three-quarters? Or, maybe, not quite?
Or go around back and sneak in from behind?
Simple it's not, I'm afraid you will find,
for a mind-maker-upper to make up his mind." [15]

Jacqueline

June 3, 2017   *6:00 p.m.*

I've done credit card scams over a dozen times. But for this one to work, I need Camille and Monica to be on point. Cedric gave me instructions over the phone.

Basically, all we have to do is flip the money we pull from these stolen credit cards at the tables, cash out, and get it over to Cedric. Easy in and out. His people are in place in the casino. So at this point, it's all about execution.

"Is everyone straight on what it is they have to do?" I say, applying a fresh coat of my favorite Mac lip glass, Angel.

It's a light warm pink that matches my Badgley Mischka pumps—my most comfortable shoe, which I need because I'll be standing for hours around four to six tables running this scam.

Comfort is key. Well, style is too, of course, which is why I'm wearing a Juicy Couture Black Label French Terry romper underneath a distressed cropped jean jacket from Urban Outfitters.

---

[15] Dr. Seuss, *"Oh, The Places You'll Go!"* verse 17

Monica is wearing a very cute halter jumpsuit of mine. Black, accessorized in silver, with black wedges. And Camille is looking sassy classy in one of my hunter green palazzo pantsuits. I have to say, I picked some cute outfits for this trip.

"One more time, please," Monica says. "I'm sure I have it, but just one more time for shits and giggles."

"No worries. You need to feel comfortable. The key is to always maintain an air of confidence. If you start to *look* nervous it'll draw attention to you and the whole shit is blown."

Both Camille and Monica are listening intently as I explain the scam.

"Remember, the goal is to stack as much money as we can without drawing attention. So for each table, play no more than four rounds," I say, drawing circles on a notepad to represent the crap tables.

"Go to the ATM; pull five hundred dollars off of the five cards." I hand both of them a stack of credit cards. "Then go to the crap tables and play: place fifty dollar bets. After four rounds, cash out. One, so you don't draw suspicion from the card dealers, and two, because you gotta try and get through as many cards as possible. They go dead after you pull off the five hundred so as not to trigger the fraud departments."

"After you've played four rounds, we'll meet up and I'll give you another stack of cards."

Camille grabs her charm and rubs it.

"How will I know which table to go to?" Camille says.

"You can go to any table, it doesn't matter," I say. "You're using somebody else's money. Just win big."

"Hopefully lady luck is on your side: you win, you tap out.

In the event you are being watched, they'll see that you're pulling out more money from the ATM and will just think you're blowing through your paycheck. That's it!"

Monica nods.

"Camille, you good?" I say.

"Yeah." She mumbles. "I got it."

I turn to look at her.

"Camille?"

Camille looks at me. "I'm good."

"Okay great. Let's meet back here in four hours. After everyone cashes out, we'll take a taxi to Cedric's. Once there, we'll give him the money, he'll give us our cut, and then we can go hit the outlets and really celebrate our graduations! Nothing should go wrong tonight, it's an easy scam. Which is why I like to do these."

"You do credit card scams regularly?" Camille says, her nose turned up in the air.

I almost snap my neck turning to face her. "Bitch, you wasn't complaining when it got you on that plane or in this penthouse."

"I never asked you to do any of that, Jacqueline," Camille whispers.

"Yeah, but you certainly didn't turn it down," Monica says, bouncing her right leg over her left as she lounges in an oversized chair in the corner of the sitting area.

Camille and Monica lock eyes.

"I was scared. I didn't know . . ."

"You knew, Bitch. You knew your name wasn't Estelle or Marguerite or whatever the fuck the name was on those credit cards." Monica slowly stands. "But yo good-at-playing-innocent ass wanna act like you all high and mighty now?"

Camille rolls her eyes. "I never said I was high and mighty, Monica. Don't transfer your insecurities about swinging on a pole onto me--"

Monica takes off, and before I can process what's really going on, she's on top of Camille pounding her.

"Moni!" I scream.

She can't hear me because Camille is screaming and wailing at Monica. Well, actually at air, because she never lands a punch. But Monica is fucking her up.

"Stop it!" I say, pulling Monica off of Camille. She's still swinging and kicking.

"Fuck that stuck up, Bitch! We do all this shit to save her sorry Bitch ass and she got the nerve to judge you and say she didn't ask you to do it? Are you fucking kidding me?" Monica tries to swing, but I catch her hand. "I will beat that Bitch's ass. Ungrateful stuck up, Bitch."

Camille sulks in the corner of the chaise lounge. She tries to pull her messy hair up into a bun. Her face is red and tear-stained. Her clothes disheveled.

Monica walks to the other side of the room and starts shuffling through her travel bag. "Let her ass figure out a way to get back home, Jay. She don't need you or your stolen credit cards." Monica glares at Camille from across the room. "Mommie or Daddy can send for her."

"They can!" Camille screams. "And so can Jacqueline's parents. And that was all I was saying. She has the means, or at the very least access to means." Camille looks directly at me. "All I was asking was why were you doing it when clearly you don't have to? You have money."

"It's not about the money, Cam." I rifle through a few outfits. "It's about the rush; like today. Making shit happen from nothing. The thrill of getting away with it."

Camille is staring at me like I have two heads.

"I do it because it makes me feel alive."

"At the expense of others?" Camille whispers.

"Yes! At the expense of others, Camille," Monica says. "Because in the real world there are winners and losers. If yo game is tight, you win. If yo shit is raggedy, then you lose."

"But those people's shit wasn't raggedy, Monica. Somebody stole their information. They're probably hard working people. And you just spent their money on a twenty-five hundred dollar a night room!"

"*We.* Not you. *We. We* are in this room, not just Jacqueline," Monica jumps in. "Why you tryin' to act like you don't have anything to do with this?"

"Moni, it's cool."

"No, it's not! We should have left her ass in New York. Let her explain how Marcus ended up sprawled out on his bathroom floor with his head bashed in," Monica says staring at Camille.

"I am grateful," Camille says, staring at the floor.

Monica grunts. "Well shit, if this is gratitude I'd hate to see if you were being *un*grateful!" She rolls her eyes.

"Okay, okay," I say, walking over to Camille. "Back to your corner, Contender," I say with a wide smirk.

Monica rolls her eyes and flips me off.

Sitting next to Camille, I pull her thick hair off her face. Dried tears leave mascara-smudged streaks down her cheeks.

"Are you going to be okay tonight?" I say in a soft whisper. "They're expecting three of us. Are you going to be able to do this?"

Camille looks up into Monica's glaring eyes. "Yes. I'll be fine," Camille says.

"Okay, great." I let out a deep sigh. "Because Cedric ain't no base ass nigga. He spent a lot of money to get us out here and set up. Crossing him would not be the business." I turn to look at myself in the mirror. I pull overgrown bangs behind my ear and pucker my lips. "He wouldn't have a problem sending us home completely dismembered and stuffed in a suitcase."

"Um, and . . . you're okay with that? I mean, you're working for a killer, basically, right?" Camille says.

"Basically," I reply. "But if we do our part, get him what he wants, then we're good. I've never had any issues before," I say as I apply a fresh coat of lipstick. I rub my lips together, pop them, then turn and explain the scam.

"Gamble a little, at a crowded table so people can see you lose.

Then, after you lose, go to the cage and get a five G cash advance on the card. They can run the cards, they're legit; the strip works and everything. Put all but one hundred in your bag. Take that hundred back to the tables.

"When you lose again, go back to the cage. When the card reaches its max for cash advances, the cashier will tell you the card was declined. Act sad and shit, and then take the card, and walk the fuck up out the casino."

Monica

I stand at the end of a crowded craps table, where the minimum bet is one hundred dollars.

"New shooter!" The Craps Dealer yells

I take two dice from the pile and shake them in my hand. I look tentatively at Camille who smiles nervously. A man with a heavy Texas accent, standing to my left, reassures me.

"Don't worry honey, with your looks, ain't no way you can lose!"

I place a one hundred dollar chip on the Pass Line, take a deep breath and roll the dice. Seven. Everyone around the table cheers. I throw another hundred-dollar chip on the Pass Line.

I roll the dice. Seven again. Everyone around the table cheers even louder. The crowd grows bigger. I place my last hundred-dollar chip on the Pass Line. I roll the dice. They bounce off the back wall. Eight.

"The point is eight." The dealer says.

"Keep it coming you lucky girl. I'm betting with you!" The man from Texas drawls. He places five hundred dollars on eight the hard way.

I shake the dice, look up toward the heavens to say a quick prayer, and roll the dice. Seven. The crowd utters their disappointment. The dealer sweeps away everyone's chips.

"I guess you win some and you lose some." I say to the man from Texas. He smiles at me as he places another bet.

Me and Camille leave the table and head to the cashier's cage. We show our credit cards and get cash advances of three thousand dollars each. We hand all, but one hundred dollars, to Jacky.

We go back to the tables, and after losing a couple of times, head back to the cage. With each cycle, I grow more confident.

Camille is looking lost at a table, standing next to two men in huge cowboy hats howling at the moon every time they roll the dice. I catch Jacky's eye; she gives me a small nod and tips her head toward the casino exit. I nod and turn to get Camille's attention.

As I walk past her table, she doesn't notice me. The second time I walk behind her and tug her blouse. She turns to the right and then the left where she sees me walking toward the exit. Camille collects her chips from the dealer and heads toward the door.

I glance over at the cage as the cashier hands Jacky her credit card. She shakes her head and says "Sorry," placing her care on the counter. Jacky reaches for the card. But before she can pick it up, the cashier quickly grabs it off the counter and picks up her security phone.

While I'm watching Jacky at the cage, I see three security officers heading in her direction. I pull out my phone and text her.

"5-0 to your right!"

Jacky turns and casually walks behind the cage to her left and heads for the door. I start to make my way to her direction, but she sees me and shakes her head. I stop and make a beeline in the opposite direction.

I see Camille a few feet behind me. I nod toward the exit and she nods and heads that way.

From my vantage point, I see the security officers closing in on Jacky. She makes a quick turn to the left and out of nowhere double doors fly open. A mob of people files out into the aisle right behind her. I look up, Club Paradise.

The officers fight their way through the constant flow of drunk and high millennials as Jacky breaks into a trot the last fifty feet of the casino. But just as she is about to approach the exit, a female officer grabs her arm from behind.

Fear covers Jacky's face. She jerks free, and bolts for the door, but the cop grabs her purse and the strap breaks. Jacky makes a dash through the door.

Two minutes later, as I'm pushing through the heavy glass door, I hear someone leaning on a horn, screeching tires, and then, screams.

"Oh my god!" a woman shouts. "Someone call an ambulance!"

I push through the crowd to find Jacky laying in front of a taxicab. Her eyes are wide open. For a split second, I think she's looking at me, and I wait for instructions – surely this is a part of the plan. But I quickly realize the blank stare doesn't change and she isn't moving.

I bend down, grab her cell phone and take off.

"Did she just steal that poor woman's cell phone?" an old lady shrieks.

As I pass the revolving door, Camille is making her way around and out the door. I am running full speed and don't even acknowledge her. I can see she's confused, but when she turns to her right and sees Jacky surrounded by security guards, she takes off after me.

We turn behind the hotel, run two blocks and into the parking structure of the adjacent hotel. Two more blocks and onto the bustling Las Vegas strip where we slow to a casual pace and blend into the crowd coming off the outside escalators from the MGM.

As my breathing starts to regulate, I can hear the thoughts in my head. *Fuck! Jacky is dead. Jacky is dead!* I turn to look at Camille; she's walking like a zombie, tears streaming down her face, a huge glob of snot oozes over her top lip. I yank her to the side of the street, out of the foot traffic.

"Wipe your fucking face," I bark. "You're going to draw attention to us by walking down the street looking like you're mentally challenged and lost!"

Camille doesn't reply. She doesn't make eye contact. She just stands there, with tears streaming down her face.

I take the tail of her shirt and wipe her face, then turn and storm off. Camille follows behind like a lost puppy.

What the fuck do I do now? My mind is racing . . . I stop and turn, Camille runs into me. I grab her arms and look her in the eyes.

"How much money do you have?" She doesn't reply. I shake her hard. "Camille! How much money do you have?" Again, blank stare. I grab the tote from off her shoulders and rifle through it.

"Fifty-two dollars? Is that all you have?"

She nods.

"Fuck! I have the fifteen Gs from the casino plus a little from my set at the club last night, but we're short thirty from you and Jacky."

"Let's go home, Monica," Camille whispers. "Let's call our parents and tell them to come pick us up." She rubs her temples. "I can't do this anymore."

"Well, Bitch! You don't have a choice!" I'm in her face now. "Do you want your parents to end up dead? He knows who we are, remember? You can't just jump on a plane and bail. We've got to square up – you heard Jacky." A knot forms in my throat saying her name. "Cedric ain't one to be fucked. And I don't know about you, but I ain't trying to arrive back home in fifteen pieces."

Camille grabs the pendant around her neck and rubs it absentmindedly. "How much do you think we owe him?"

"I don't know how much profit he was expecting. But if he's okay with just the amount we took off the cards, about fifteen thousand."

Camille slides down the wall until she hits the pavement.

"Jacky was killin' it at the tables. I wonder how much she had in her purse?"

"What are we going to do?"

"We can't get back into the room; Jacky had the key in her purse. We can't produce IDs in the names on the room if they ask us to show proof of who we are," I say, pacing back and forth, talking it through.

I pull Jacky's phone out of my pocket. Scroll through her recent calls, and click on Cedric's number.

"Hey Cedric, it's Moni, Jacky's friend."

"Why you calling me? I don't know you," he says.

"I know. I'm calling you because Jacky is dead."

I explain to him what happened and told him how much money me and Camille had left. There was a long pause on the other end of the line.

"Sucks to be you right now, doesn't it, Mami?" Cedric says.

"Yeah, it does," I say. "And I can't pull a couple of g's out the air, if you know what I mean?"

"Yeah." He pauses. "Take down this address and get here by eight. You and the L7 do this one solid, y'all be straight."

"What are we doing?" I ask.

"Making me whole." The phone goes dead.

I look over at Camille. She's doing that stupid rocking thing again, rubbing her charm.

"We need to go get Jacky. Call her parents . . ." Camille says.

"We need to make sure we don't end up dead. You heard what Jacky said about Cedric," I say, cutting her off.

"She was just . . . laying there . . . dead," Camille says, rocking back and forth, staring into space.

"Listen, they are going to contact her parents who are going to fly up here and retrieve her body."

"How? Her I.D. says she's someone else. And she had over a dozen credit cards on her."

"True. And once they see that, they'll just use her dental records to identify her. That's what detectives are for."

Camille nods and continues to rock.

Two of the closest people to me are dead. This is some crazy shit. I say to myself.

CHAPTER THIRTEEN

Hot on the Trail

"But on you will go
though the weather be foul.
On you will go
though your enemies prowl." [16]

Detective Morales

June 3, 2017   *2:30 p.m.*

"You got nothing, Washington?"

"No, Detective Morales. No activity on Monica Lopez's cell in forty-eight hours, sir."

"What about her friend?"

"I checked her Facebook page. There are two posts with her and two other females"

"Good job, Washington. Send me those photos."

I hang up and wait for Washington's text. Standing in front of the Tropicana hotel, I look down the street at all the tourists walking up and down the busy Las Vegas strip. A group of drunk teens hoots and hollers as they bob and weave in and around the other people doing much the same.

Swoosh.

The photos come through. I closely inspect their faces. None of these girls looks like they'd fuck around with Marcus. One looks like money, one looks super innocent, and this other one – she has to be

---

[16] Dr. Seuss, *"Oh, The Places You'll Go!"* verse 29

the stripper. She is beautiful, but I can see she's lived a little. Not like the other two. This one's eyes are hard. Even her smile seems to hide something. But she is definitely beautiful. Boricuan. Those mixed-breeds have an exotic look to them. They have all the best of both races. This girl definitely does.

Everyone said she was smart.

"Let's see how smart." I stroll the strip looking for the trio.

Monica

June 3, 2017   *7:00 p.m.*

"Moni Love." Cedric eyes me in a way that makes me uncomfortable.

"Hey Cedric," I say to the huge glob of a man. He has to be over three hundred pounds. But he is tall as fuck. He towers over us as we stand in the middle of his office.

"Fucked up what happened to your girl," he says with absolutely no emotion at all. "It's been all over the news." He stares at Camille.

Tears are streaming down her face. I pray that she doesn't start to rock.

I just nod in response. I feel like my throat is closing. Jacky was my only female friend. Girls could never get past my exterior to get to know me well enough to become my friend. All of a sudden, I feel so completely alone.

"So whut up, sho'ty tho?" Cedric says, pausing to breathe deeply as if those five words depleted his entire air supply.

I hate deep breathers. My uncle Tito who stayed with us for six months is a deep breather. He slept on the couch in the living room, so I had to turn up the T.V. extra loud to hear it.

"You tell me. We're here to square up."

"Whatchu got?"

"All we got is fifteen thousand." I lay the money on the desk. "Jacky had your money. She was calling the shots."

Cedric stares at us emotionless.

"Looks like y'all got problems then."

"You said you been watching the news, right? Did they say she had your money and credit cards on her?"

Cedric looks me up and down. I pray to God they reported that on the news. Camille and I had hightailed it out of there and never looked back; I didn't know what they were reporting.

"There's a party up at my homeboy's mansion in a couple of hours. Y'all can make me whole." He pulls open a desk drawer and takes out a long metal case, opens it and pulls out a Ziploc bag full of pills. He tosses two bags across the table.

I grab them.

"There's sixty pouches of E in each bag. Two pills in each pouch." He looks over at Camille who's still crying. "You should be able to blow through these in no time. The ballers pop these like after dinner mints." He chuckles revealing sparkling gold fronts.

I nod.

"Yeah?" he says.

"Then we straight?"

"Yup."

"Bet."

"Aiight. I'll get Tone to drive y'all up there." He pulls his phone out and sends a text. "He's the shot caller on site. He's going to introduce you to my client who will tell you how he wants his clientele approached." Cedric sits back in his chair.

"Don't fuck up my shit."

Detective Morales

June 3, 2017   *5:30 p.m.*

I flash my badge at the redhead behind the counter. She stops short of rolling her eyes. Instead, she flashes me her biggest smile.

"How may I help you sir?"

"Detective Morales, ma'am."

Her left eyebrow inches up. "Detective Morales, is that a New York accent I hear?" She loosens, her fake smile turning genuine.

"And you picked that up from me saying my name?" I grin, leaning in. "You're good," I whisper.

The red in her cheeks starts to travel down her neck, which she instinctively covers with her right hand. "Thank you. I *am* good." She tosses back, even though it makes the red in her cheeks splotch. She clears her throat. "I pride myself on being able to identify which regions of the country my guests are from before they hand me their IDs," she says, beaming with pride.

"Oh yeah?" I say pulling out the photos of the girls. "You wouldn't have happened to check in these New Yorkers, would you?"

She examines the picture. "No, I'm afraid I haven't, Detective." She hands me back the photo.

I slide it back inside my jacket pocket. Shit, this was the eleventh hotel I'd been to. No hits. I was beginning to wonder if these girls were really here or if that post on Facebook was to send the police on a wild goose chase.

I turn to face the lobby. They probably were in Mexico somewhere.

"Is there anything else I can help you with, Detective?"

I turn back to face the redhead, she's giving me that — you can have it if you want it — look.

I pause, checking her out. I'm guessing she's around twenty-two or three—she's white, her rubber-looking chest suggests she lays out regularly, so I don't know for sure—she could be younger.

The left corner of my mouth inches up. Once again, she blushes. I weigh my options. I don't hurt for pussy. If I want a good hand job, I slide Miko a rock. I don't go up in her anymore, not even with a condom. But her hands – she gives the best hand job in the Bronx.

I can always fuck my son's mother, Annalisa. Even though she's got the best pussy I've ever had, it comes with too much mouth—and not the kind that goes around my dick. It's the kind that Bitches and complains about the fucking sun rising and setting every day.

I usually just get a girl from Bonnie. Her girls are high end. Bonnie services elected officials and Wall Street suits, so I don't have to worry about my shit falling off or waking up in pain.

I look at the redhead and my boy starts to rise, letting me know he's definitely interested in some freaky sex. White girls love fucking *us*. They get to go buck wild and break free of all the 'behaving properly' constraints they live under every day.

But just as I'm about to get my mac on, the redhead points to the flat screen in the lobby.

"Detective, isn't that one of the girls in your picture?"

I turn to see a picture of a beautiful, young African American flash up on the screen. The caption reads: "Recent New York Graduate: Jacqueline Roberts, hit by Taxi". I walk closer so I can hear the details. The reporter says next of kin have been notified and that police are interested in speaking with anyone at the scene who has any information about the incident or the victim.

I pull out my cell.

"Washington, I have another name. Jacqueline Roberts." I walk toward the exit. "Yep, cell, social media - same as before. Send me whatever you find."

I hang up and dial the number listed on the screen.

CHAPTER FOURTEEN

The Big Payback

"You'll be on your way up!
You'll be seeing great sights!
You'll join the high fliers
who soar to high heights." [17]

Monica

June 3, 2017   *7:30 p.m.*

I watch the sun make its slow decent behind the Nevada mountains as we snake up the private two-lane road. The sky turns from a soft blend of orange, fuchsia and golden yellow—reminding me of my middle sister's favorite ice cream, a Big Stick—to a dark blue blanket speckled with stars. What I'd do to be able to go to the bodega and buy her one right now.

Camille is sitting up under me even though we're the only two in the back of the black Escalade. From my peripheral vision, I see her tear ducts still producing at full force. But I'm not mad as I struggle to fight back the tears pounding on the back of my eyes and push down the howl threatening to explode inside my throat. I just want this shit to be over so I can go home.

We drive the twenty-minutes up the winding road that takes us deep into the hills. We arrive at two massive iron gates that slowly open to the most magnificent mansion I've ever seen in my life. It's more fabulous than the million dollar homes on HGTV. Tone pulls the

---

[17] Dr. Seuss, *'Oh, The Places You'll Go!'* verse 9

Escalade around the palm tree lined-circular driveway. A huge, brightly lit, water fountain commands the center of the driveway. Large streams of water shoot about 6 feet high into the sky and cascades down into a large pool.

As we walk up to ornate double wood doors, Camille grabs my hand and squeezes it.

I look back at her and force a smile.

"These things will sell themselves. We'll be home before you know it, Cam," I whisper.

She nods and tries to smile, but tears stream down her cheeks instead.

Inside, a short Mexican wearing a white tuxedo leads us up one of two long staircases. As we walk up the left side, I can't help but stare at the massive chandelier hanging between the two staircases. The iron and crystal – there has to be over a hundred pieces.

We turn left and walk down a long hall, past at least ten rooms on each side to a red door in the back of the house. The butler opens the door and lets us in, but doesn't go inside.

On the other side of the red door is a massive room.

There is a billiard table, a kitchen and bar area with black granite countertops; an under-counter refrigerator, and two dishwasher drawers.

We step down past the bar into what couldn't be less than a five thousand square-foot basement area that creates a third sub-level. It includes a wine cellar with wine racks that holds what looks like at least thousands of bottles of wine.

A movie theater is next to the wine cellar. It has a projection screen system with surround sound and nine cushioned easy chairs.

An exercise room is next to the movie theatre, as well as an elevator that connects all three levels and ascends to the second and third levels above the basement. Or, you can climb a terra cotta stairway with iron railing.

"You like it?" a booming voice comes from behind a sliding glass door. In walks the tallest, finest, best-dressed brother I have ever seen in my life.

"I do," I say.

He smiles broadly. "Thank you." He closes the glass door behind him. As he steps down into the basement, I see behind him a shitload of verandahs, including a stone gazebo, two fireplaces, outdoor kitchen and sunken bar.

Water cascades from a Jacuzzi down into a vanishing edge swimming pool that includes multiple fountains shooting out vertical streams of water.

"You won't find many homes in Las Vegas like this one," he says, walking toward the bar. "It's a classic Mediterranean-style Italian villa. It's the only custom-built of its kind in Southern Highlands Country Club. I bought it with my signing bonus."

My stomach drops thinking about Jacky. Knowing this is the type of home she'd be living in, decorating, hosting parties in, filling with babies with her basketball husband who'd probably look like this guy.

"Mr. Johnson. These are our girls for tonight. Moni and Cam." Tone says.

The baller nods.

"So what's the run down for tonight?" I say, done with his bragging.

"Tonight, your job is to keep my friends happy." He smiles as he extends his long arms. "I'm providing all of the entertainment. Including ah . . . a little jump start to get them to that happy place."

I nod, so he knows that I understand what he's implying.

"You'll make your way discreetly around and simply ask folks if they want to Get Happy. If they say yes, you make the transaction. If they say no, you keep it moving. No hard sales, you understand?"

"I do."

"Okay, great. Cedric and I have been doing business a long time, so I don't foresee any problems. You do your job; you make a lot of money. My friends like to be happy." He chuckles. "You," he says, pointing at Camille, "can work the outside. And you can work the inside." He hands us both neon green, pink and yellow necklaces and bracelets. "They'll be looking for these. So, don't trip if someone comes up to you and says I want to get happy."

We nod, and take the neon ropes.

115

The first hour of the party is slow. The basketball players are mostly drinking Crown Royal and Hennessy. The groupies are drinking whatever is being served and smoking weed around the infinity pool— no smoking is allowed inside—but plenty of lines are being done on every flat surface of the house.

I spot Camille walking around outside and head over to her.

"How's it going?"

"It's not," she says, looking down. "I just don't feel comfortable pushing someone's drugs. People overdose on ecstasy!"

I grab her arm and pull her to the side. "Camille! You better come down off your high horse real quick. Have you forgotten that we have no money? Have you forgotten that if we don't sell all of these pills tonight, Shamu the whale is going to have Tone Loc put a bullet through our heads?"

Camille's eyes grow big.

"Nobody is putting guns up to these peoples' heads and making them use this shit. They are adults, and trust me; this is not the first time they've taken ecstasy." I drop her arm and get up in her ear. "Now, sell your stash so we can get the fuck up outta fucking Las Vegas and get the fuck back home!"

Camille mad dogs me for a moment, then straightens up and walks off. "If I never see this place again in my life it won't be soon enough." She approaches a couple on a chaise lounge chair. "Hi, you guys want to get happy?"

Detective Morales

My visit to the Las Vegas Metropolitan Police Department is a colossal waste of time. After speaking with the homicide and sex crimes bureau detective, Captain Letkiewicz, for over an hour, bringing him up to speed on the connection between the Roberts death and Williams death, I still got nothing.

"I'm sorry, Detective Morales. At this point in the investigation, all we can share with you is that we've notified the next of kin and they're on their way to claim the body."

"And I'm telling you she's connected to a homicide in New York City that took place less than twenty-four hours ago." I show him photos of Marcus' crime scene.

"Yes sir. I understand. And I'd like to help you, Detective. But I have no new information at this time. The most I can do is put you in contact with our public information officer who has prepared a press release and YouTube video about the incident—if there's anyone who would have any more information, it would be Director Alston."

"So, your public information officer would have more information than the detective assigned to the case?" I put my hand up and shake my head. The fact that they only have one detective assigned to homicide and sex crimes should have been my indicator that I wasn't going to get very far with this slapstick police department. *A press release and YouTube video?*

Detective Morales

June 3, 2017   *9:30 p.m.*

Back on the strip, I dial Washington to see if either of the two girls have used their ATM, credit cards, or cell phones.

"No sir," Washington reports. "But Jacqueline was busy posting pictures to her Facebook and Instagram."

"And?"

"And the last photo has the Ritz Carlton logo in the background."

"Anything else, Washington?"

"No, sir. The other picture doesn't have any identifying landmarks—it's just a close up of the girls."

"Good job, Washington." I say and swipe my phone closed.

Fuck! I spit. "Where are you?" I say out loud to the girls I can't seem to find.

I came up empty at the Ritz Carlton. The manager went back three weeks and couldn't find a registration under any of their names. I showed their pictures to everyone on duty—which was useless seeing as though they had changed shifts about three hours earlier.

I walk the strip, looking, thinking, and trying to get in the minds of these girls. Jacqueline had a shitload of money and credit cards in her possession. Did they each have their own stash? Were they working other casinos? Or, had they found a connect here and sold my shit?

I stand in front of the Luxor hotel looking out onto the strip. From what I can deduce, Jacqueline was the ringleader, and probably the one with the connections. But did she, Monica, and this third girl have anything to do with Marcus' murder? And did they have the street smarts to unload two kilos without getting jacked? If it was me, I'd just pop them and take the drugs.

I take a long drag on my cigarette. I can't figure out what their next move will be. Where they could be now. And how I'll get back that stolen evidence. The last thing I needed was that shit being traced back to me.

Across the street, neon lights flash: Girls, Girls, Girls! Nude. *Or, maybe . . . Monica Lopez is doing what she does best to make some money?* I follow my hunch and walk across the street into the strip club.

Monica

June 3, 2017   *11:30 p.m.*

Two more hours and the party starts to pick up. The ballers are drunk off their asses and the groupies are circling like vultures.

I can't keep up with all the people wanting to *get happy* inside the sunken living room; but I'm smiling and stuffing twenty, fifty and hundred dollar bills into the fanny pack Tone gave me. There are pockets on the outside for easy access to the pills and pockets on the inside to safely stash the money.

The DJ is on the third floor in an alcove in the middle of the two winding staircases. Two levels below that have been transformed into dance floors and beautiful half-dressed women with weaves down their backs are bumpin' to the music while men cop free feels or grind up against their taut big asses.

"Time to make a drop," Tone says into my ear. "Follow me." I follow him into one of the restrooms off to the side of the entertainment room. He counts the money I collected against the remaining pills I have in my pouch.

"You doing good," Tone says handing me another pouch of ecstasy. "Where's your girl? She should be needing to lighten her load too."

I nod. I had been so busy trying push my shit, I wasn't checkin' for Camille.

"I'll go find her," I say and head outside toward the infinity pool.

The music is blarin' and bodies are smacking--people are practically fucking standing up, around the pool, in lawn chairs, and cabanas. I guess Camille's been handling her business because these people are all over each other.

Two or three people who I've sold to inside, approach me for more. *Where is Camille? Why were these people from outside coming inside to get their E?* The whole point was to have one of us inside and one outside so people wouldn't have to look for us.

Twenty minutes later, I find Camille sitting in a corner near the bar on the lower level terrace.

"Uh," I say, looking left and right. "What are you doing, Cam? Tone is looking for you to cash out." She doesn't look up. "Camille?"

Still, nothing. I walk up to her and snatch her fanny pack out of her hand.

"Are you fucking serious right now?" I scream. Camille hasn't sold *anything.* "I've been inside busting my ass trying to sell all my shit so we can square up and get the hell out of here, and you haven't sold shit?" I'm so heated I forget we're at a pool party with other people. "Do you want to end up dead? Do you want to get the fuck home? I cannot do this shit all by myself, Camille. You have to do this shit, too!"

Camille slowly shakes her head and starts rocking back and forth, tears streaming down her face. "I can't. I can't do this."

I slap her so hard she falls back and out of her chair. She lets out a scream so loud people on the second level turn to look. But I'm so mad I don't give a fuck. I pounce on her and straddle her. I sock her in her face over and over. She's screaming and scrambling to get from under me. But her small petite frame is no match for the wide hips that has her pinned to the ground.

Just as I pull my fist back to punch her in the nose, a hand grabs my wrist. Then I'm yanked up off of her. It happens so quickly I'm disoriented.

"What the fuck is you doing, Bitch?" Tone says through clenched teeth. "You trying to fuck up our shit? This is our shit. Classy shit. Not no hood ass nigga shit, Bitch."

Before I can regroup and respond, the baller appears. He's wearing white linen pants, a white silk shirt, and brown sandals.

"Is there a problem?" he says to Tone, looking from me to Camille who has crawled over to the edge of the pool out of swinging distance.

"No sir. No problem at all," Tone says, smiling. "I was just telling the hired help that this is an upscale classy event, and--"

The baller holds his hand up and Tone stops talking.

"Is there a problem?" the baller says to me.

I look in Cam's direction; she turns away.

"She's been laying out here in the cut and not handling her business--"

"That's not our client's concern," Tone says. "I'll take care of it, sir."

The baller sips the Hennessy from the short glass in his right hand. "What about you, Boricua." He juts his chin in my direction. "You handle yours?"

I look over at Tone who is mad dogging me, daring me to speak.

"Yeah. I handled my business and apparently some of hers, too." I place my hands on my hips. "Have you been getting any complaints?"

"No. Everyone seems to be quite *happy*," he says, smirking.

I give him a half smile, proud of my accomplishment, despite Camille's disappearing act.

"But that's not the point, is it?" His face goes serious. He looks at Tone, turns, and walks away.

WTF? I turn to face Camille, but she's looking at her feet like a got-damned Re-Re. When the baller is safely out of hearing distance, Tone turns on his heels.

"You Bitches want to get shot tonight? Cuz it ain't nothing for me to put a bullet straight through your skull – fucking with *my* money."

Camille's eyes widen.

Good! Maybe now she understands the seriousness of the situation. She can't just decide she's not going to do something just because she doesn't like it. Damned spoiled brat. Welcome to the real world.

Tone's phone rings. He swipes it and turns away. After a series of yeahs, uh huhs, okays and got its, Tone hangs up the phone.

"That was Cedric." He motions for Camille to come close. She moves quickly to where we are. "He's pissed as shit. He just got off the phone with his client." We both look at Camille. "Let's go."

We follow Tone up the two outside levels, the three inside levels, and this time down the hall to the right. Midway down the hall, Tone stops and points to a door. "Boricua, you go in there."

I hesitate, but slowly grab the doorknob. "Shit for brains, follow me."

I smile and walk into the room.

Camille was shit for brains. I don't know what else I need to tell her, but *Dorothy, we ain't in Kansas no more.* Values and judgment have no place in the land called survival. If she don't wake the fuck up she's going to get herself killed. I won't be going down with her stuck up ass. She can be stuck up and dead if she want to be. Moni don't play those reindeer games.

In the 'hood, you square up, pay your debts, and don't fuck around with other people's shit. Camille don't know this, of course—her parents take care of all her problems. She'd better wise up, and quick, or she is going to find herself on the end of a bullet that could care less about some morals.

The room is the size of my dance studio back in high school. The hardwood floors and mirrored walls make me think of it instantly. But there's a bed twice the size of a California King in the center of the room. It's obviously custom made to accommodate the 7' 7" basketball player. As I step down into the massive space, Cedric waddles out the bathroom across the room. I'm surprised, but don't let it show on my face.

"What's up, Boricua?" Cedric says in between deep breaths.

"Handling my business. Your clients tell you?"

"Tone told me yo gurl ain't sold shit." He coughs. "That wasn't the agreement. Y'all need to make me whole."

"I'll sell her part. Give me a couple of hours."

"Nah," he says. "This ain't no fucking Burger King. You don't get to have it your way."

My stomach drops. "Where's Camille?" I say eying the door.

"That Bitch is in a broom closet with a sock shoved in her mouth. She won't fucking stop crying so I made Tone shut her punk ass up."

I watch him slowly make his way over to the corner of the room. "She lucky I didn't pop her ass. But I know that was JayRo's lil homie and shit."

I slowly release the air I was holding, afraid Cedric had killed Camille--mostly because I knew that meant I was going to be next.

"So I have one last proposition for you. You do this; you and Baby-Cry-a-Lot can walk. Our score will be settled."

"What is it?"

Cedric hits the light switch. The room goes dark. Music pipes in through the surround sound: a rap song by Snoop Dog fills the room. Cedric hits another switch and the pitch-black room is illuminated by shimmering stars on the ceiling.

The basketball player appears from another door on the left. He has his glass of Hennessy in one hand and something else in his right.

Cedric motions for me to meet him at the bed. "You make my client here happy, and we straight."

The baller walks over to the oversized bed, slides back onto it, takes a sip of his drink and watches me as I walk toward him.

"Dance for him," Cedric commands.

No problem, I have a dozen routines I can pop out without thinking twice.

In the background, Snoop sings:

When I met you last night baby
Before you opened up your gap
I had respect for ya lady
But now I take it all back

I turn my back to the baller and slowly bend over at the waist. I reach and pull my hair loose from the bun on top of my head and shake it free. I pull the romper down over my shoulders, my waist, and let it drop to the floor. As I step out, I turn so both Cedric and the baller can see me standing in my bra and underwear.

I read Cedric's lips, *Oh Shit!* He reaches his fat hands into his baggy jeans.

I turn to face the baller and he's already got his hard dick out, stroking it. He motions for me to come close, but I do my most sultry turn, bend again at the waist, and wiggle my ass in his direction. Through my spread legs, I see him smile.

I can't think quickly enough on how to get out of this situation.

So, I hook the sides of my panties with my thumbs and pretend like I'm about to pull them down. Instead, I drop down into a split and bounce up and down slowly. I toss my hair over my shoulder and bite my bottom lip as I move up and down. Both Cedric and the Baller increase the speed of their strokes.

Cedric and I meet eyes. He nods in the direction of the bed. I pause because I can't help but think of Jacky. This is her scene. This is her man. My stomach turns as I slink across the floor until I'm in between the baller's spread legs.

He opens a small plastic pouch, takes out a pill, pops it in his mouth, and chases it with Hennessy. He takes out another pill and offers it to me.

I smile and shake my head. But he insists. I look over at Cedric who nods. I open my mouth and he lays the pill on my tongue. He hands me the Hennessy and I sip.

Cedric pipes up the music. "You remember this shit right here baby?" He raises his glass.

Guess who is back in the motherfuckin house
With a fat dick for your motherfuckin mouth

The baller looks over at Cedric and bursts out laughing.

"Hell yeah!" he shouts, grabs a fist of my hair and pulls my face up to his dick. He shoves it in my mouth and moves my head up and down, each time faster, harder. No stranger to a blow job, I expertly maneuver my mouth around his shaft, over the tip of his head, followed by a strong hand gripping and stroking him as I work the 10,000 nerves on his head.

"Oh shit!" he moans, his eyes roll to the back of his head. "Yeah!"

I sneak a side view and Cedric is about to climax as well. Two more minutes and he will blow. But just as I'm bringing him in for the pop off, he pulls me up off my knees, up on the bed, and slides me down on top of him.

My head is spinning, the room is hot, and I've never felt anything as good as this dick inside me. I slide down hard, banging my butt against his hips. But no matter how hard I pound, it just doesn't go in deep enough. My whole body is on high alert, no matter where he touches, it comes alive. It feels so good.

Now it feels as if he is an octopus. He has two hands, four hands, six hands – the numbers keep growing as I feel him touching every part of my body. My breasts, my butt, my mouth, and my neck – how can he touch so many places at once?

My mind is reeling, my body is floating, and I'm hungry for more. I pop up and down; twirl my head around and around. His hands are squeezing my breasts; his mouth is covering my mouth. Then he's pulling me back and now his dick is in my mouth, and inside my pussy, and inside my hand and I'm stroking him—but I'm sucking him, and I'm fucking him . . . the room is spinning . . . I force my eyes open . . . to focus.

There are a dozen men surrounding me. I can't make out their faces, but I can see that they're naked. Light skin, dark skin, white, tall, short . . . I can't gain control of my body though I'm fighting with all my might. It's moving in all kinds of directions. Being pulled and prodded, but I can't . . . do anything . . .

I open my mouth to say stop, but it's filled with something warm and gooey. I look up and see a dark chocolate six-pack blocking my view. He moves to the left and I see Cedric. I try to scream for help, but the words won't form in my mouth. I try to focus and all I can do is lay there and listen to the words of the song playing in the background.

It ain't no fun, if the homies can't have none
It ain't no fun, if the homies can't have none
It ain't no fun, if the homies can't have none

Monica

"Monica. Monica. *Monica!*"

It sounds like I'm under water. There's swishing in my head, but I think I hear my name.

"Monica, wake up!" I'm being jerked back and forth.

"Wake up!" *It's Camille.* I look up into Camille's big eyes. Damn her eyes are big as fuck.

"Monica, please. Please wake up!"

Slowly I come to. I strain and focus.

"Let's go. Hurry."

I try to move but can't. I look down and see a big ass Asian man lying across my body.

"What the--?"

"Here, I'll help you." Camille pulls as I push the mass of a man off my thighs. As he falls to the hard wood floor making a hard thump, I look down and realize that I'm naked.

"Here." Camille shoves my clothes in my hands.

I slide into the romper and scan the room for my shoes.

As I step into the last shoe, Cedric starts to stir. My adrenaline kicks in.

"Let's go!" I say, heading for the door.

Camille is on my heels. We take the stairs three at a time. We round the corner and take the back stairs down two levels.

Outside, it's pitch black and the party is still going strong. Girls are stark naked dancing, jumping in the pool, and making out on every area of the patio. Everybody is high and happy; it's one big outdoor orgy.

We find the parked cars and I start checking for unlocked doors.

"Find an unlocked car, Cam," I shout.

After several attempts, the door to a cobalt blue 550 Mercedes Benz opens. "Here! Let's go." Before Camille can get good in the passenger seat, I've hotwired the car and am half way around the circular parking lot.

"How are we going to get out?" Camille screams as we approach the gate.

But before I can answer, the gate starts to open. Automatic exit. *Yes!* I gun it out the gate and down the winding road.

Thirty minutes later, we're in an alley behind a 7-Eleven, wiping down the 550 with some lotion I found in the glove compartment.

"I don't understand why we can't just drive this home?"

"One. We probably wouldn't make it out of Nevada. He's got less than a half of tank of gas. Two. They've probably reported it stolen by now, and if not, will soon. We don't need to add GTA to the list of shit we've already done in the past seventy-two hours." I pause and give her directions. "Hit every place you think you may have touched, Cam."

She nods and rubs every surface area she can find. We leave the car and head toward the strip.

For twenty minutes, we blend into the crowd. Cam is following me as I walk and think, trying to come up with a Plan F. Because clearly Plans B – E went seriously wrong in the worst way.

As I walk, my body feels as if it's coming down off of anesthesia. All of a sudden, I feel pain shooting through my vagina. It's like someone took the stickiest type of masking tape they could find, laid it on the inside of my vaginal walls, and pulled it—ripping all the skin off.

The pain is worse than the worse eyebrow waxing I've ever had—when the wax was too hot, and I let my hair grow too thick. It's worse than the one fucking time I got a Brazilian wax. When Marcus got released from prison and I wanted to be silky smooth. That shit hurt so bad; I slapped that Bitch and got kicked out the salon.

My shit is so tender it's excruciating to walk. I stop at a bus stop and sit. I can't remember shit, but based on how my body is feeling, I know the train they ran on me must've been long. My pussy is so beat up, it feels like my insides are about to fall the fuck out.

"Monica," Camille says, scraping dried up, Lord knows what it is, off my neck. "Are you okay?"

I don't reply. Mostly because I'm in so much pain I don't have the energy; but partly because this shit was her fault. If she had sold her stash of the *E,* we could have paid Cedric's ass off and been on our way home.

Now we're back to square one—no money, no plan, and so far from home I could--

Splat! Camille jumps back just in time. I miss her shoes. But just as quickly another wave hits, and then another, and another. Before I know it, I'm dry heaving. My body is trying to get rid of all the bile from this weekend. There's nothing left, yet I don't feel empty of the shame, guilt, and sadness.

Plan F is quickly shaping up to be Plan *Fucked.*

CHAPTER FIFTEEN

Plan F

"You'll come down from the Lurch
With an unpleasant bump.
And then the chances are, the,
That you'll be in a Slump." [18]

Monica

June 4, 2017   *6:00 a.m.*

"Monica," Camille says in almost a whisper. "I think it's time we call our parents."

Though it nearly rips my insides out, I turn abruptly to face Camille. "You think it's time we call our parents?" I place my hands on my hips, tilt my head to the side, and give her the nastiest glare I can muster. "Okay, go call Mommie and Daddy, Camille," I say pointing in the direction of the nearest hotel. "And what are you going to tell them?"

"The truth!"

"Which is?"

"Which is . . ." She looks from side to side. "Which is Marcus' death was an accident, but we freaked out and left town . . . and Jacky's death was an accident, but we-we- we were scared. And. Ended up – no, we were forced to go to the mansion . . . And. Oh my god!" Camille slumps down on a nearby wall. "It all sounds awful."

"And unbelievable, right?"

---

[18] Dr. Seuss, *"Oh, The Places You'll Go!"* verse 14

"Right." Camille stares down at her feet. "But we need to get home." She's in full on tears. "How are we going to get home, Monica?"

I'm tired, dirty, and hungry as shit. I don't have the energy to comfort the reason why I'm in this situation in the first place. But I know she can't think her way out of a box.

"I don't know about the Coleman's, but Yolis and Victor ain't no fools. The first thing they're going to do is ask why we didn't call the police? Why we fled instead? How we got to Vegas, and how Jacky ended up dead . . ." I rub my temples.

"I told you to call the police!"

"And we were trying to save your ass, Camille! All of this shit was to protect *you* from going to jail for bashing in Marcus' head. Why does that little fact always seem to escape your memory?"

"It doesn't. But if we had just explained it to the police--"

"Camille! Seriously? You're black. Do you know that?"

Camille's face twists into a frown. "Of course I know that."

"Really? Because you say we should have called the police as if you believe we're innocent until proven guilty?" Camille gives me a blank stare. "Well we're not. We're Black. They throw Black people up under the jail." I shake my head in exasperation. "They don't give a fuck about us, or if we're innocent. They're on a mission, and that mission is to incarcerate as many people of color as they can. Men, women. They don't care. Why the fuck you don't know that is beyond me." But I know why. Camille has lived a sheltered life in upper Manhattan, believing that the shit the poor people go through don't apply to her.

"Do you have any money on you?"

Camille nods and pulls out forty dollars. "My only sale of the night."

I snatch the two twenties and we walk over to the ninety-nine cent store. I spend five dollars on some black leggings, a leopard print thong, an oversized leopard t-shirt, a pair of big gold hoop earrings, and a tube of red lipstick. Camille spends another five dollars on a cotton sundress, a pair of flip-flops, deodorant, toothpaste and a toothbrush.

We have breakfast at Denny's, then wash up and change in the restroom. And it's there I share with Camille my plan to get us home.

But first, we need to get some sleep. We find a twenty-four hour Wal-Mart, locate the camping section, and sneak into one of the tent displays. We're asleep for less than four hours when two security guards pull us out of the tent by our feet.

"Word of advice," the manager says. "The next time you decide to hide out in a display, try not to snore like a damn Harley Davidson."

The security guards laugh as they escort us out the door.

Detective Morales

June 4, 2017   *6:00 a.m.*

"There are more strip clubs in Vegas than hotels," I say to Washington, rubbing my eyes. "Who knew?" I'm tired and need to shower and shave.

"It ain't called Sin City for nothing, Detective." Washington chuckles. "I assume you didn't come across anyone who saw the girls then?"

"Nah," I say, lighting up a cigarette. "Or if they did they weren't telling."

"Why wouldn't they tell?"

I stare at the cityscape. In the midday sun, it looks like most metropolitan cities, but at night, people reinvent themselves here. From Elvis to Madonna, from big ballers to arm candy, from the most expensive escort to the twenty-dollar hooker, they become somebody completely different.

"Because they wouldn't want anyone to tell where *they* are." I sigh. "They're missing because they want to be missing, Washington. There's loyalty on these streets. Or, at the very least, respect for the game."

"So what are you going to do?"

Just then, a call comes through. "I'll call you back Washington, it's a seven-oh-two number, it's the police department." I switch over. "Detective Morales."

The detective says he just got a call from the Theft and Vandalism department about a GTA. Says the description of the perps match the two girls I came in looking for. I take down the address and hail a cab.

"I need to go to Southern Highlands Country Club."

"I already told the detective all I know about the stolen vehicle," the owner of the mansion says, slouching back in a black leather recliner.

I take in the massive home. Mexican workers are cleaning what was obviously a wild industry party. Red cups, empty liquor bottles, and half-eaten party trays litter the grounds. I eye the basketball player.

"Yes sir, I understand, and I apologize for asking you again . . . but the Las Vegas Police Department alerted me about the stolen vehicle because the description of the perpetrators match those of two suspects I'm searching for in connection to a homicide in New York City.

"*New York City?*" two security guards say at the same time, like the 90's Pace Picante sauce commercial. They burst into uncontrollable laughter.

The basketball player chuckles, "Yeah, sorry. I don't know how I can help you. I was inside hosting my guests. You're welcome to speak with the valet, he was the one who saw them and made the report. They staff all my parties – but, like I said, *I* can't help you, Detective."

"So, you don't think they were attending the party? You think they somehow flew in clear across the country, made their way up that private road, and passed that fortress, onto your estate – just to steal a car?" I look into the basketball player's eyes.

He shrugs and stands. "I don't think anything. I told you what I know. Now, if you'll excuse me, I have practice tomorrow. I need to get some rest. Sean will show you out."

The fat-necked security guard stands and walks in my direction. I flip my notebook closed. I raise my hand and turn toward the door.

In the cab, I call Washington. "Do your Facebook thing again, Washington. Check and see if you find any pictures of Monica or the other girl at that party last night. I'm sure some groupies were snapping pictures. Maybe they caught one of the girls in one of them?"

Monica

June 4, 2017   *12:00 p.m.*

It's twelve in the afternoon. Usually the time club managers are making last minute changes to the night's line up.

"How can I help you?" the sweaty Italian club manager says in between puffs on his cigar stump. There are sweat stains under his arms.

I've cut the neck and shoulders off the t-shirt so that it hangs just enough to show my mounds and tan skin. I took off the skirt to accentuate my full bubble in the skintight leggings.

"I was hoping to get in a set tonight," I say.

The manager looks up over his clipboard and removes his horn-rimmed glasses. "You were hoping, were you?" he says, looking me up and down.

I turn, and give him a good look at my butt. He smiles.

"Where you from?" He leans back on the podium.

"I'm from wherever you want me to be from, Daddy." I toss my hair, letting him know I ain't no rookie. I know how to create a fantasy.

His smile widens. "Yeah, okay. So then you know we already got our regulars lined up for tonight--"

"Them old tired ho's? They ain't got nothing on me." I roll my eyes. "Let me at least show you a routine. Then if you don't like what you see, I won't waste any more of your time." I step up on center stage. I turn my back to him, but turn at the waist to look in his direction to see if he gives me the okay. I toss my curls over my left shoulder and place my hands on my hips.

"Okay." He chuckles. "Let's see what you got. What song?"

"Whatever your favorite song is."

Another smile. He yells up to the DJ who puts on an old eighties classic, *White Horse*.

I laugh. And drop down into a straight split, bouncing up and down slowly as if I'm riding a dick.

All the men in the club shout, "Whoa!" and clap.

I roll over on my stomach and crawl toward the pole in the center of the stage. Before I inch up the steel pole, I discreetly wipe the tears from my face. My body drops and pops instinctively doing the routines I've mastered over the years as a limber dancer and expert stripper, but the pain is searing through me. It feels like I'm being ripped in half from the inside out.

As I turn to face the mesmerized crowd who've stopped to watch, I fight through the pain and smile, seductively, licking my full red lips, and cupping my breasts. As I move toward the pole the music stops.

"Okay, okay!" the manager says. "No freebies. You guys can come back tonight and see--" He looks at me.

"X'Stacy." I cringe as I repeat my stage name.

"Yes." He smiles wide. "You can come see Ecstasy perform tonight. Bring your big bills, fellas. This ain't gone be no dollar show."

I smile and sashay off the stage.

Detective Morales

June 4, 2017   *11:00 a.m.*

I receive a text from Washington: *Check your email.*

Bingo! She is in the background, but there she is. Monica Lopez.

What is she doing? WTF? It looks like someone is sliding hermoney. Is this Bitch selling my dope?

"Mutherfucker!"

Could she move that much shit on her own? She must have connects here in Vegas. But she wouldn't be moving it herself, would she? Maybe her thing was high-end parties. She could move it fast and probably get top dollar for it.

But that's not smart business. Smart business is cutting it and tripling the supply, selling it to crack heads who don't know the difference—and could care less—about high quality. They just need a hit.

"Fuck!"

Monica

June 5, 2017   *12:00 a.m.*

The Guido tells the girls I am his niece from New Jersey to prevent a revolt. They let me borrow some pieces to make up a costume.

I do my routine to Amy Winehouse's "You Know I'm No Good" and rock it! It is an older crowd, which is good for me. Older cats get more into the fantasy because usually they can't get their shit hard no more. And, they have more disposable income than the younger ones, and usually big bills.

Inside the cab on the way to the airport, we count the money.

"Shit Moni!" Camille says, recounting the stacks after I count them out a second time. "We have enough to buy tickets back home!" For the first time in seventy-two hours, Camille cries tears of joy.

CHAPTER SIXTEEN

Home Sweet Home

"...for people just waiting.
Waiting for a train to go
or a bus to come, or a plane to go
or the mail to come, or the rain to go." 19

Detective Morales

June 5, 2017   *12:00 a.m.*

"What's up, Washington?"

"Sir, we got a hit!"

I toss my cigarette to the ground and quickly pull out my notepad. "Where?" I'd spent the past hour canvassing the area around the 7-Eleven where they dumped the car looking for witnesses.

"They just purchased tickets at the airport under their legal names."

"Where are they headed?" I step to the curb to hail a cab.

"Back to New York, sir."

"I'm headed to the airport now--"

"If you can't get there in twenty minutes, then it'll be too late. Looks like they just boarded Southwest Flight 1913 to LaGuardia."

I can hear Washington clicking on his keyboard. "They land at six thirty a.m."

"Have a squad car waiting for them when they step off the plane, Washington."

---

[19] Dr. Seuss, *'Oh, The Places You'll Go!'* verse 19

"Yes sir!"

"I'll head over to the precinct as soon as I land. Washington?"

"Yes sir?"

"Do not let anyone interrogate them, do you understand me?"

"Yes sir!"

Monica

June 5, 2017   *1:17 a.m.*

As the plane tilts left, Camille's head falls on my shoulder. I look down at the toothbrush in her hands, the only memento from the past seventy-two hours, besides the haunting nightmares that kept me up the entire five-hour flight.

One dream was of Marcus. Half his head was bashed in, his wife beater was covered in blood. He had the same blank stare he had lying on his bathroom floor, but he was alive and screaming at me.

"You never loved me! You used me from day one. And you never wrote me one letter or visited me once while I was in the pen."

He was spitting—not saliva, but blood. And by the time he finished screaming in my face, it was completely covered in red.

Another dream was of Jacky. She had the same blank stare she had lying on the ground in front of the taxicab. She was combing her hair in the mirror, and when she turned to face me, her ribs were protruding from her favorite Michael Kors jump suit.

"You just left me laying there. I would have never left you like that. You were supposed to be my girl. I always looked out for you, don't you remember? When everyone else treated you like garbage; I always had your back."

The tears won't stop pouring. Twice, the flight attendant hands me napkins. But it doesn't matter. They won't stop coming.

I don't know if I've cried as much as Camille has this past weekend, but if I haven't, I surely come in a close second.

By the time the plane lands at LaGuardia, my face is so swollen, Camille gasps when she wakes up and sees me.

"Monica!" She covers her mouth. "I think you're having an allergic reaction or something. I can barely see your eyes." Camille goes to push the button for the flight attendant, but I grab her hand.

"I'm fine," I whisper.

"No you're not," she says.

"No. I'm not," I say. "But since when has that mattered?"

The "fasten your seatbelt" light comes on and the flight attendant asks everyone to power down their electronics. I have never been so happy to go home in all my life. I can't wait to walk up my street, the stairs to my brownstone, and into the cramped three bedroom.

I can't wait to be in the same room with my sisters. As a matter of fact, nothing sounds better than being in that room breathing the same air as Annabel and Marisol and fighting for the covers, or five minutes alone in the bathroom. *Nothing.*

We exit the plane. But we don't get ten feet before we're surrounded by ten officers, guns drawn. I freeze. Camille bumps into me.

"Monica Lopez?" an officer says, grabbing my arms and placing them in handcuffs behind my back. "You're under arrest for the murder of Marcus Williams."

The blood leaves Camille's face as she's cuffed and Mirandized.

Detective Morales

June 5, 2017   1:45 p.m.

"Sir," Washington greets me at the precinct interrogation room. "They're in interrogation rooms one and two."

I nod.

"Coleman has asked for an attorney. Lopez isn't saying anything."

I walk into the room where Monica Lopez is. Her wild curls fall down her back and over her shoulders and onto the table. She's fallen asleep, her face inside her folded arms.

"Ms. Lopez?" I pull out a chair across from her. "Good morning. I'm Detective Morales. How are you?" She doesn't say a word, just stares at me as if I'm speaking Chinese. "Ms. Lopez, you are being charged with the murder of a Marcus Williams. If there is anything you'd like to tell me, now would be the time."

I wait for two full minutes. Nothing.

I flip open the manila folder, pull out a photo, and slide it across the table.

"You can start by telling me what it is you're selling at this party?"

She turns her head to look at the picture. Her expression doesn't change.

I reach over and point to her taking money from one of the people at the party. "So now we have a motive. You kill your boyfriend, steal his drugs, and go to another state to sell it." I eye her.

She chuckles and shifts in her chair. "Drugs? I know cigarettes kill, but the last time I checked they weren't illegal. Certainly not classified as drugs. Did I miss some new legislation, Detectives?"

"Cigarettes. Really?"

"Really. She overpaid for them, but that's what you do when you're hard up at a party. I don't think it's a crime to capitalize on that."

I grab the picture; slide it back in the folder. "Okay, have it your way." We lock eyes as I stand up to leave the room. There's no fear in this girl's eyes.

She's been around the block a time or two.

CHAPTER SEVENTEEN

The Have's v The Have Not's

"And when you're in a Slump
You're not in for much fun.
Un-slumping yourself
Is not easily done." [20]

Monica

June 8, 2017   *9:00 a.m.*

"All rise," the bailiff shouts. Everyone, but the judge, stands. "Department One of the Superior Court of the State of New York is now in session. Judge Richard Price presiding. Please be seated."

"Good morning, ladies and gentlemen. Calling the case of the People of the State of New York versus Camille Marguerite Coleman and Monica Aracelie Lopez. Are both sides ready?"

"Ready for the People, Your Honor," the district attorney says.

"Ready for the defense, Your Honor," the public defender replies.

The doors of the courthouse swing open, and in struts a force of a woman wearing five-inch patent leather heels, that puts her at about 5'8" tall. The red two-piece suit looks painted on, showing off her amazing hourglass figure and even more amazing, muscular legs. Her peanut butter complexion seems stark against her shiny black bob and swoop bangs that draw your eyes straight to her full red lips. She flips her hair back.

---

[20] Dr. Seuss, *'Oh, The Places You'll Go!'* verse 15

"Your Honor, I apologize for the interruption." She walks into the gallery like she owns it. "Zahra Cosner for the defendant, Camille Coleman."

The public defender turns to face the woman. The judge looks up over his reading glasses.

"Mr. Jacobson, were you aware of a request to separate the case?" the judge says to the public defender.

"No, Your Honor, this is the first I've heard of it."

The attorney holds up a document. "Yes sir, that would be because I have the filed papers here. I just had them processed ten minutes ago."

The bailiff takes the document and hands it to the judge. He flips through the papers.

"And so you have." The Judge looks up and nods toward the district attorney. "I take it you have?"

"Yes, Your Honor. The people have no objections to granting severance in this matter."

"Objection, Your Honor, based on what grounds?" the public defender replies.

"On the grounds that a joint trial precludes the calling of the codefendant who may have exculpatory evidence. The United States v. Echeles, 1965."

"I know the ruling." My Public Defender rolls his eyes harder than any Bitch I've seen roll her eyes. "Your Honor, Echeles moved for a severance in order for the codefendant to testify on his behalf."

"The public defender is correct, Your Honor." Ms. Cosner hands the bailiff another set of blue backs. "We are requesting severance on the basis that, among other things," she eyes the public defender, "there are conflicting defense strategies. A joint trial would compromise the trial rights of my client and prevent the jury from making a reliable judgment about her guilt or innocence. There is evidence against the codefendant that we will be introducing during the trial that could prejudice the jury against my client."

"Request to approach, Your Honor?" the public defender says.

"Approach the bench, Counselors."

The public defender, Ms. Cosner, and the district attorney approach the judge who is reading over the documents the lady attorney handed him.

I watch Ms. Cosner stroll easily to the bench. That was going to be me in the courtroom: demanding respect and turning these arrogant ass men on their backs. I smile, watching Ms. Cosner work. But my smile fades as my public defender returns to my side.

"What's going on?"

The judge looks up and over his reading glasses pronounces, "The defendant, Camille Coleman's trial will run seriatim with the trial of codefendant, Monica Lopez, so that the defendant is not denied due process. The state, in order to ensure a trial free from prejudice, will conduct separate trials simultaneously in different courtrooms."

"The judge severed the case," the public defender says, packing up his briefcase. "The trial starts in two weeks."

🎩🎩🎩

It takes my public defender four days to come to see me and explain what the fuck is going on. After he dropped that bombshell about Camille testifying against me, her attorney requested bail. Four minutes later, I was being escorted out the courthouse and back to my jail cell and Camille was being taken to processing, and released on bail.

I can't believe this shit. She kills Marcus, and I'm the one going down for it? All the shit I did to save her ass, and she's pinning it on me?

"Camille killed Marcus. Not me."

"Great. What proof do you have?"

"Me and Jacky were at the club. She called us and said he attacked her. He was dead when we got there."

The attorney takes notes as I recount the entire weekend.

"Wow," he says, sitting back in his chair, scratching his chin. "That's not at all how Camille tells the story."

"Fuck how she *tells* the story, what I'm telling you is the truth."

The public defender slides his note pad inside his briefcase and closes it shut. "And what I'm telling you is that your truth doesn't matter right now unless you have proof."

Damn, if Jacky were alive, all of this would be a non-issue. She'd tell them the truth. Not some version of the truth.

But right now the truth wasn't helping either one of us.

Monica

June 20, 2017   *1:30 p.m.*

Two days before I take the stand, mi familia come to visit.

My mom is devastated. She loved Jacky, and listening to the testimony of everything she was involved in blew her mind.

"Prieta, why are they saying such ugly things about Jacky? She was a good girl."

"She was a good girl, Ama. You've watched enough *Law & Order* to know that they have to say these things to win their case."

My mom nods wanting desperately to believe me. She clutches the handles of the Tori Burch purse Jacky gave her.

When my mom leaves to use the restroom, Papi looks me in the eyes and say, "I knew she was boosting those purses."

We just stare at each other. I can't lie to my dad. It's like his eyes are made of kryptonite or something. He nods and looks away.

"I knew Marcus was a piece of shit, but why didn't you tell me he was laying hands on you, baby girl?" My dad's eyes become shimmery from the liquid welling up inside.

"I didn't just lay down and let him beat me. You know we went toe to toe," I joke. But it doesn't take away the pain behind my dad's crooked grin.

"My job is to protect you. Maybe if you had told me, you wouldn't have ended up here." He looks around the beige visiting room. Everything is dirty and steel. "I know you got to do what you got to do, but it almost killed your mom hearing that you were a go go dancer."

I chuckle. Even now, my dad only sees the best in me. I love him so much. I love the way he always looks at me with hope and pride. Even now.

"So, the DA is offering you a plea bargain?"

I roll my eyes. "Yeah. But I didn't kill Marcus, Papi. Why would I accept seven to ten when I didn't kill him?"

Papi nods, but he doesn't look me in the eyes.

"I know, baby girl. I believe you, of course, but you can't guarantee the jury will." He rubs his goatee the way he does when he's trying to figure out a solution to a problem. "That girl has a high powered private attorney." He pauses. "You know if I could afford one, baby girl--"

I grab my dad's hand and smile. "I know."

And I did. If he could have given me the world, he would have. That just wasn't the life we lived. "But if I take a plea, I'll have a felony and then I can never go to law school. That was the only reason I worked at that club, Papi. To get through undergrad so I can go to law school. You know becoming a lawyer is the only thing I've ever really wanted to do."

My dad smiles and squeezes my hand. "I know, baby girl. I know."

Monica

June 21, 2017   *9:30 a.m.*

"Will the clerk please swear in the jury?" the judge says to the bailiff.

"Will the jury please stand and raise your right hand? Do each of you swear that you will fairly try the case before this court, and that you will return a true verdict according to the evidence and the instructions of the court, so help you, God? Please say, "I do".

"I do," the jury says in unison.

"You may be seated."

The deputy DA stands up and speaks to the jury.

"Your Honor and ladies and gentlemen of the jury: the defendant has been charged with the crime of murder in the second degree.

"The evidence will show that Ms. Lopez, in a fit of jealous rage, bludgeoned to death the victim, Marcus Williams with a metal baseball bat.

"The people will show that the defendant, Monica Lopez, was the mastermind behind covering up the murder. Not only is the defendant's fingerprints on the bat used to bash in the victim's skull, but there's motive, opportunity, and an eyewitness who will corroborate that she, in fact killed, Marcus Miller in cold blood. The evidence I present will prove to you that the defendant is guilty as charged."

Monica

"The prosecution may call its first witness," the judge says

"Thank you, Your Honor. The People call Camille Coleman to the stand."

Camille is escorted to the witness stand. "Please stand. Raise your right hand. Do you promise that the testimony you shall give in the case before this court shall be the truth, the whole truth, and nothing but the truth, so help you God?"

"I do," she says.

Camille is wearing a knee-length navy blue A-lined dress, donned with white and pink flowers.

"Please state your first and last name. And spell your last name for the record."

"Camille Coleman. C-O-L-E-M-A-N."

Camille's hair is flat ironed straight and pulled back by a thick white headband. The sandy brown hair flows down the middle of her back.

"You may be seated."

The Deputy DA stands up and walks toward the witness stand.

"Please state your occupation for the jury."

"I am a freelance photographer, but my paid job is as an assistant curator of photography and art for the Gavin Wright Gallery in lower Manhattan."

"So you are a recent graduate?"

"Yes. That's right. Liberal Arts major, from NYU."

"Congratulations." The DA walks back toward his table. "Now, could you tell me where you were the night of May eighth?"

"Yes, I was at Sin and Seduction."

"Could you tell the jury the nature of the business and why you were there?"

Camille lowers her head and whispers, "It's a . . . strip club."

"I'm sorry. Can you speak up so the jury can hear you, Ms. Coleman?"

"A strip club," she repeats, louder. She looks completely mortified. Camille turns to face the jury. "I was there . . . because Monica. Well, she worked there, and . . . Jacky and I were . . . we were going to meet up there and celebrate our graduation." She drops her head and clutches her neck.

"You look, uncomfortable speaking about Ms. Lopez's occupation, Ms. Coleman." The deputy DA walks back to the witness stand. "Why is that?"

"Objection."

"On what grounds, Counselor?"

"Relevance."

"Mr. Lexington?"

"Background, Your Honor. To establish the character of the witness."

"I'll allow it. The witness will continue."

"I don't go to strip clubs," Camille says in a strained voice. "I only went because Jacqueline . . ." She becomes choked up.

The DA walks over and hands her a tissue.

"Thank you." She dabs her eyes. And wipes her nose. "Ahem, I only went because my best friend, Jacqueline pretty much begged me to go."

Camille looks over at me and we exchange cold stares.

"And did you know the decedent, Marcus Williams?"

"Yes. I was his high school sweetheart." Crocodile tears flow. I roll my eyes.

"That is, until of course, until Monica transferred to LaGuardia." Camille looks over at me and smiles.

The DA turns to face me, pausing for affect.

"And then what happened?"

"Well . . . and then Marcus and Monica started dating."

"He stopped dating you and started dating Monica Lopez, just like that? Did he tell you why?"

"Yes. He told me he loved me, but I was a devout Christian then, and practicing abstinence." Camille looks over to the jury. "I was saving myself for my husband." Camille's cheeks turn red. She straightens out her dress. "And he . . . well, he was a normal high school boy with raging hormones."

"And Ms. Lopez wasn't abstaining?"

"Objection!"

"Withdrawn."

"Careful, Counselor."

"Yes, Your Honor. Ms. Coleman, please explain to the jury how you ended up in Mr. Williams' apartment on the night of May eighth."

"Well, when I got to the club, Marcus was in a screaming match with the bartender."

"What were they arguing about?"

"He wanted another drink, but the bartender refused to serve him."

"What was your opinion of the state Mr. Williams was in that night?"

"Oh he was drunk." Camille chuckles. "He was staggering. And I struggled to keep him standing. But he wrapped his arm around my neck and I held him up as best I could. I held him up around his waist and got him out of there before that bartender killed--" She gasps mid-sentence. She brings her hands up to her face and sob.

The DA hands her more tissue. "I know this is very difficult, Ms. Coleman. I'm sorry."

She wipes her nose. "No, it's okay. I understand." Camille looks sheepishly in the direction of the jury. "I'm so sorry."

A female juror looks like she's about to break into tears, another's eyebrows are furrowed and her mouth is turned down.

"I told the bartender to tell Monica I was taking Marcus home."

"So you struggle, but you get him to his apartment, and then what happens?"

Camille nods. She dabs her nose again with the tissue. "Well. I pretty much dump him on his bed, and fall out next to him because by now, I'm exhausted."

"And then what happens?"

"Nothing. We just lay there and Marcus thanks me for looking out for him." Camille looks up and stares out into space. "Then he says, 'like you did when I first came to LaGuardia.'" Tears stream down her cheeks. The DA hands her more Kleenex. "And then he just, starts to reminisce." Camille blows her nose. "He starts to recount how we met, and all the things we did together, discovered together, how we were so in love."

"Then what happened?"

"Then I got up. I told him I didn't want to talk about the past. He made his decision and we were adults now, so . . ."

"What was his response to that?"

"He sat up. Grabbed my hand and pulled me back down to the bed." Camille turns to face me. "He said he was a stupid kid with raging hormones back then. But he never stopped loving me, never gave his heart to anyone else." She turns to face the DA. "He told me he never stopped loving me."

I shivered at her words and just stared at her. "Please tell the jury what happened next, Ms. Coleman."

Camille drops her head.

"We made love." It is barely a whisper.

"Can you repeat that please, louder so the jury can hear you?"

"Um." She blinks a few times. "We made love. Marcus kissed me. He looked me in my eyes and told me he loved me, he never stopped loving me—and I said I'd never stopped loving him." Camille looks into my eyes. "Because it was true. I had never stopped loving him. And, we kissed. It felt...natural. My lips remembered his, and his remembered mine.

"Before we knew it, we were naked and in each other's arms— making love." Tears stream down Camille's face.

The DA walks slowly over to the witness stand and waits for her to compose herself. "And then what happened?"

Camille wipes her now red and swollen face, and blows her nose.

"Then we heard keys in the door, and before we could move, Monica barges in." She is looking at the jury.

"She, she was screaming 'You lyin', cheatin' N-word!' He was on top of me and she rushed him, but he shoved her to the side. He jumped out of bed and I pulled the covers up around me. He grabbed his pants and slid into them. She got up in his face. They were arguing."

"Did she say anything to you?"

"No. She never said or did anything to me. The most she did was look at me." Camille drops her head and fumbles with her Kleenex. "We weren't friends or anything like that, but I did kind of hang out with her from time to time because of Jacky." She glances over at me again and I want to tell her stop staring, stop lying, Bitch!

"All Monica did was look at me. More like glared at me and said, 'You finally made your way back to this 'B—'.'"

"What happened next?"

"Marcus got angry and told her not to call me a 'B—'." Camille fumbles with her fingers. "He told her she was the 'B—', a dumb 'B—' 'that swung on a pole and pumped her 'A—' in old men's faces for a dollar." She looks at the DA. "That's when he walked into the bathroom. The last thing I heard him say was 'You're a tired 'A—', washed out dollar ho.'"

"That was the last thing you heard him say? What happened when he walked into the bathroom?"

"He walked into the bathroom, made that statement. I'm reaching for my clothes when all of a sudden, Monica grabs a bat from the corner of the room and runs into the bathroom screaming 'Eff you! You weren't saying that 'S—'when you was punching on me like a punching bag and crying, beggin me not to leave your sad sorry 'A—'!" Camille is crying and shaking uncontrollably.

The judge says, "Ms. Coleman, would you like to take a break?"

She shakes her head. "No. I'm sorry, Your Honor. I'm fine."

"Very well then." He nods to the DA. "Continue with your line of questioning."

"Thank you, Your Honor." He walks up to the witness stand, and very gently says, "Please tell the jury what happened next."

"I hear Monica screaming that stuff about being a punching bag, and then I hear this . . . I guess the best way to describe it is like a dull thud. And then this loud crash, which was Marcus falling to the ground."

"Did you see Monica hit Marcus, or see him fall to the ground?"

"No. I just heard it."

"What did you do?"

"I jumped off the bed and ran over to the bathroom."

"And what did you see?"

"I saw Monica holding the bloody bat over Marcus' lifeless body. Blood was forming into a puddle around his head." Monica shakes her head. "He wasn't moving."

"What happened next?"

"Then Jacky ran into the room." I gasp.

I can't believe Camille is bringing Jacky into her lie. But I see what she's doing—sneaky bitch. She's indirectly creating another eyewitness. I want to jump up and charge over there and beat this bitch's ass.

"She stood behind me." Camille says. "She looked at Monica and said, 'My god, Monica, what the "Eff--' did you just do? Is he dead?'

"Monica dropped the bat like she was in a daze or something and pushed past me and Jacky and ran into the bedroom.

"She sat on the bed and started crying into her hands like this." Camille puts both her hands up to cover her face. "She said, 'I killed him.'"

One jury member is shaking his head. Another juror has his hand over his mouth. All I can do is shake my head as I jot down some of her lies on a yellow notepad. It is hard to keep track of all of them, though.

"What happened next?"

"I slid into my clothes and went for my phone."

"What were you going to do?"

"Call the police, of course."

"But what happened?"

"When I pulled out my cell, Monica jumped up and snatched the phone out of my hand. She said, 'What do you think you're doing?' I told her 'Calling the police. Marcus is dead!' She said, "You ain't calling 'S—'! I'm not going to jail over this piece of 'S---'"

"How did you respond to that?"

"I sat down in a chair. I mean, she had just killed Marcus in cold blood--"

"Objection!"

"Sustained."

Camille turns to face me, pauses, then speaks in a very calm voice.

"I was scared for my life. Monica wouldn't let me call the police. I essentially was the only witness. I didn't know what she was going to do to me."

"What did she do?"

"She got up and started grabbing things."

"Grabbing things? Like?"

"Like, his Bose system, his Rolex – you know, expensive things around the apartment."

"For what purpose?"

"She said, 'Start grabbing some stuff so they think he was robbed and killed by some crack head."

"Marcus Williams was a drug dealer?'

"Allegedly," Camille replies, looking away from the jury. "Remember, I hadn't been with him since high school. I don't know what type of lifestyle he led at this point in his life. I just foolishly believed him when he said he still loved me." Camille turns to face the jury and gives them a quick, weak smile.

"It all happened so quickly. One minute, I'm helping Marcus up the stairs, the next we're making love, and then, he's lying in the middle of his bathroom with a pool of blood around his head." Camille dabs the corners of her eyes. "I never understood what they meant by a crime of passion. But Marcus' death was just that: quick, violent, and out of nowhere. Monica must have snapped."

"Objection, Your Honor. Please ask the witness to only testify to those things that are within her knowledge and expertise."

"Sustained. Ms. Coleman, please only answer the questions asked."

"Yes, Your Honor. I'm sorry."

Camille tells the rest of the story exactly how it happened, with us dumping Marcus' stuff in dumpsters across boroughs, Jacky making a call, us going to Vegas. All of it, she recalls as it unfolded.

"So explain how you can fly across the country, sleep in the same room with the defendant for seventy-two hours knowing what you knew? How come you didn't call the police? Or try to escape?"

"It was weird . . . those seventy-two hours are like a blur to me. I was there but, it was like I was floating, going through the motions," Camille says, as if she was talking in a daze right then.

"I trusted Jacky. She was my best friend. And, I didn't believe that Monica set out to kill Marcus. It just . . . happened." Camille turns to

the jury. "Honestly, I think seeing me and Marcus together in bed--"
She looks at the public defender, then carefully and slowly says the
next sentence, "I think seeing us, and then hearing Marcus say all those
mean and spiteful words were just too much."

"Too much for Monica?" the DA says.

Camille looks over at me and gives me the most pathetic look.
"Yes."

"Thank you, no further questions, Your Honor."

Camille's testimony lasts three days. One day for the district
attorney to present, and two days for my public defender to cross-
examine.

My public defender tries to poke holes in Camille's testimony. But
says without corroborating evidence, it is all hearsay.

Witness testimony corroborates Camille and Marcus leaving
together, and me and Jacky leaving together. Camille's version of the
story is that I charged over to Marcus' in a jealous rage because the
bartender told me he left with another woman. Both of us say Jacky
was trying to find parking and came in after everything takes place.

Because Camille called Jacky on her burner phone, there is no trace
of the call. Jacky never came upstairs, so even if she was alive, she
wouldn't be able to contradict Camille's account that she walked in the
bathroom and saw me standing over Marcus holding the bat. It literally
comes down to Camille's word versus mine.

The DA brings in expert witnesses. One says it sounds like Camille
suffered from Stockholm syndrome and had obviously experienced
feelings of trust or affection toward her captor during the apparent
hostage taking.

Another expert presents data that shows how people can be in
shock and physically do things but are checked out mentally and
emotionally because the mind is functioning in a protective state. His
last expert says it is plausible that Camille was functioning from a place
of fear, that her adrenaline basically kept her in motion and doing

whatever she needed to do in order to stay alive. Either scenario provides an explanation as to why Camille is a victim, not an accomplice, and certainly not the mastermind.

I wear the black Armani pantsuit Jacky gave me for my graduation. True to form, I was wearing it for my first trial. Who would have thought then I would be the defendant and not the attorney.

I am on the witness stand for five days. The public defender questions me for two days, establishing, what I believe, is a pretty solid case against Camille. I tell my version of the story—the truth--and then the DA cross-examines me for three days.

I hold my ground, don't get emotional, but at the same time I don't know if I'm emotional enough to convince the jury that I am not a cold-blooded killer.

In his closing, the public defender focuses on motives and why the motive the district attorney presented is weak, at best.

"A crime of passion is just that--passionate, emotional, irrational, uncalculated. Yet, if what DA Lexington is proposing is true, then Monica, in a passionate rage, killed Marcus Williams—but not the woman he was in the throes of having sex with when she supposedly burst in the room? So what was she, selectively passionate? It doesn't make sense.

"So let's recap the prosecution's theory: Ms. Lopez violently kills Marcus, then flies clear across the country with the only eyewitness to her crime? By the co-defendant's own admission, she went freely. She even corroborated the fact that Ms. Lopez did a number of things to protect her and keep her safe. The DA says it was because Monica either felt guilt or was trying to keep Camille quiet. But again, doesn't make sense.

"Ms. Coleman herself admits that there were several situations in Las Vegas where she could have been killed had Monica not intervened. Instead, Ms. Lopez did some pretty unsavory things to keep them both alive. Does that sound like a cold-blooded killer? Or someone who was trying to keep her eyewitness quiet? She could have permanently silenced the only witness who could testify that she was Marcus' killer. *If* she had truly been the person who killed him.

"If Monica snapped and killed Marcus in the heat of passion—then she should have killed Camille as well. What would she have had to lose? History shows us time and time again, crimes of passion are not selective or rationale – certainly not when it comes to the cheating partner and whomever he's cheating with.

"Children, sometimes? Even then, convicted murderers have confessed afterward that they snapped and weren't thinking straight when they killed innocent children. That the anger and frustration took over them, and they honestly didn't have control of their faculties."

My public defender walks to the prosecution table and stands.

"I submit to you that this story," the public defender looks down at the prosecutor in disgust, "and that is all that it is, nothing more than a sensationalized fabrication of the truth—is not to be believed.

"Ms. Lopez confirmed that Marcus had become cold and violent, so when Ms. Coleman told her he had attacked her—raped her—causing her to kill him in self-defense, she believed her.

"That's why Monica Lopez didn't kill her in a crime of passion . . . that's why Camille was smiling in the pictures on Facebook with Monica and Jacqueline Roberts . . . and why Monica protected her at the mansion. That's why Monica danced at a seedy nightclub to earn enough money to get them both back to New York—because she was not the killer!

"The prosecution paints Ms. Lopez as a cold and calculated killer because she came up with the idea to make the incident look like a robbery gone bad. But that couldn't be further from the truth. If she had been cold and calculated, she would have simply called the police. Or she would have allowed Cedric to kill Camille.

"But she didn't. Why, ladies and gentlemen? Because she had been on the other side of Marcus' rage and she empathized with Camille. In fact, she was being compassionate!

"That's why Ms. Lopez went along with Jacqueline's plan to leave the state. That's why she protected Camille at the mansion in Las Vegas. That's why she figured out a way to pay for those plane tickets back to New York. Not because she was a killer; but because she was innocent.

"No one knows what took place in that room between Marcus and Camille. It's logical that Ms. Lopez's fingerprints would be on the bat; she was his girlfriend of six years. Her fingerprints were on many items in the room, after six years you're bound to find them everywhere.

"But what doesn't make sense, and what the prosecutor conveniently glosses over is Camille Coleman's motives. You heard her, ladies and gentlemen – she was devastated that Marcus left her for Ms. Lopez. They were high school sweethearts. She never stopped loving him. She waited to give her virginity to him, even after all those years. Who had the real motive to kill Marcus Williams?

"Perhaps a crime of passion did take place on Unionport and Sagamore Street that night. But it wasn't Monica Lopez who committed it. It was Camille Coleman. She took advantage of the opportunity to be alone with Marcus that night. And maybe they did have sex. But who's to say what happened next?

"Maybe the hard and callous Williams rejected her? Maybe she thought they would get back together after all the years she spent pining for him? But what if he rejected her? And in a fit of rage, after giving up her virginity to the only man she ever truly loved, she snapped!

"Now the story makes sense. With that motive, it makes sense that the girls would scramble to protect her, would travel across the country to give her an alibi, that Monica would try and prevent her from being victimized again at the mansion, and would go the extra mile to get her back home to safety.

"Remember, ladies and gentlemen, the prosecution must prove every part of its case beyond a reasonable doubt – that means that you must be very sure.

"One of the things they must prove is that my client killed the victim, Marcus Williams. It's my client's word against Camille Coleman's. My client testified under oath that she did not kill him. She also testified that she only came up with the story of the robbery to protect Camille because she believed she had killed him in self-defense.

"The prosecution has presented no real evidence to prove that this is not true. That means that there is a reasonable doubt and, therefore, you must find Monica Lopez not guilty.

"You do the math." The public defender walks back to our table. "From where I stand, the prosecution's case doesn't add up."

Monica

June 30, 2017   *3:45 p.m.*

Eight days. That's how long it takes to change the course of my life. It's all a blur now, and those eight days feel more like seven minutes. Even though when I was on the witness stand being cross-examined by the prosecution, it felt like seven years. But right now, sitting here, waiting for twelve people to determine my future has me bugged out.

Rehashing the testimony in my head, of expert witnesses, of the evidence presented . . . watching the expressions of the jury . . . of Jacqueline's parents and her brother. What I'd give to get those seven days back.

To say something differently, wear something different, smile, or cry – anything to ensure that this moment ends in my favor. Seven days will come down to fourteen seconds when the foreman stands and reads the verdict. And my life will never be the same.

But the truth is, my trajectory changed the moment I stepped foot into Marcus' apartment that night.

"All rise!" the clerk shouts.

It takes the jury three days to deliver their verdict in my Case.

Me and my attorney stand. I scan the faces of the jury. They're all blank. I can't read any of them.

"Will the jury foreperson please stand," the judge says.

A short white man with a shiny baldhead stands.

"Has the jury reached a unanimous verdict?"

"Yes, Your Honor, we have," the foreman replies.

The clerk walks over to jury stand, gets the verdict form from the foreman, walks to the judge and hands it to him.

I watch as the judge reads the piece of paper before handing it back to the clerk. I can't read any of their faces. My stomach is in knots and the palms of my hands are so wet, I'm leaving handprints on the yellow notepad.

"The jury finds the defendant, guilty of murder in the second degree."

I can't believe my ears. My entire body goes cold. The court erupts into loud chatter.

The judge raps the gavel twice. "The court thanks the jury for its time and service. In light of the Fourth of July holiday on Tuesday, sentencing will be held Monday, at nine a.m. Bailiff, please remove the defendant. Court is adjourned."

Despite the pleas for leniency by my parents, Jacky's parents, and an unexpected letter from Marcus' mother, that blamed Marcus' death on the lure of fast money, the infatuation of material possessions, and the pull of the streets, I am sentenced to fifteen years to life.

It takes the jury less than six hours to reach a verdict in Camille's case. Not Guilty.

The killer goes free.

CHAPTER EIGHTEEN

The Showdown

"You won't lag behind,
because you'll have the speed.
You'll pass the whole gang and you'll soon take the lead." [21]

Monica

August 19, 2017   *1:30 p.m.*

"Inmate, you got a visit!" Sergeant Stafford says as he approaches the table with a group of Puerto Ricans debating the presidential election.

I look up.

"Yeah you, Lopez. Let's go!"

I wasn't expecting any visits this weekend. My parents come the first weekend of the month and my brother, the only sibling with a criminal record, comes the third weekend. Today was the second weekend.

"Who is it?"

"Do I look like your fuckin' secretary?" the sergeant replies. "But if you don't want the visit, keep asking me twenty-one questions and I'll be more than happy to cancel it."

I stand up and walk toward the building.

It's been six months since I was convicted of second-degree murder. Six months of me trying to come grips with the fact that I am

---

[21] Dr. Seuss, *'Oh, The Places You'll Go!'* verse 10

going to spend the majority of my adult life incarcerated. Caged like an animal.

As I walk across the lawn, I scan the yard and look at all the faces: hard, empty, hopeless faces.

I guess that's what will become of me, eventually. But right now, six months in—I don't fit in. I don't belong here.

Of course, if you talk to anybody up in this place, they'll say the same thing. Everybody is innocent up in here, or a victim: their daddy was a drunk, mom was a whore, brother was an addict, boyfriend was abusive, the system fucked them over . . . you name it, I've heard it. And none of it is ever anybody's fault.

At first it used to drive me crazy. I could look at half of them and know their criminal asses did it – I didn't need to know the charge, whatever it was, *they did it!* But I had to figure out a way to do this time, to become one with the fact that I would never become the lawyer I'd always envisioned.

Oddly enough, I've become what they call a jailhouse lawyer. Clearly, I never went to law school, but somehow having a degree bestows me special powers. I think it's crazy to trust someone with a Criminal Justice degree to advise you on legal matters. I mean, that's like allowing a person who works the fry station at McDonald's to be a chef in a five-star restaurant. But once they find out I graduated from college, it's a non-stop stream of inmates asking me if I can help them out with their cases.

I have to admit; there are some dumb Bitches up in here. I wouldn't say a degree makes a person any better than the next; but clearly *education* is a valuable commodity that cannot be overstated.

I am able to read. Which is basically all I do for these women, read their paperwork and tell them what it means. I am able to rationalize and make assumptions, which I don't do with any of them – because if I'm wrong, it's a beat down. And I'm not about to get my ass beat over somebody else's case.

I read the facts and report the facts. Outside of that, my response is, *I don't know, that's above my pay grade.* It's enough to keep me protected, enough to keep me neutral. Nobody cares what race you are when they need information. They care that you have a college degree and can read better than the average inmate who, from what I can tell, reads at about a fourth grade level.

Sergeant Stafford escorts me through three iron gates and to the holding area where the Correctional Officer processes me through. I walk through a long dingy grey corridor to another holding station where another CO double checks my number, then leads me to the visiting area.

I walk into the visiting room, scanning each table for a face I recognize. Nothing. I scan again, this time slower. Nothing.

I turn to face the CO when I hear, "Monica!" and see a woman waving.

Slowly, I walk toward the table in the rear of the room. The woman looks familiar, but I can't quite place her. The eyes. I know those eyes.

Just as I reach the table, I freeze.

"Hello, Monica."

"Camille. What are you doing here?"

"Visiting you, of course." Camille points to the chair.

Camille's sandy brown hair is now jet-black. It's bone straight and cut in an asymmetrical bob the length of her chin. She's wearing makeup that looks like a makeup artist from the Mac counter applied it. And her fuchsia-colored outfit is some designer-made two-piece jacket and pant set. Three-inch patent-leather heels extend out from underneath the table.

I pause, thinking I should just grab her around the neck and choke her until her body goes limp in my hands. But the COs would be on top of me before I could kill her.

No, I should yank her out of that chair and bang her head on the concrete floor, over and over. I should be able to kill her before anyone can reach me.

At least that way, my fifteen to life will be for a murder I actually committed. I would spend a few months in the SHU (Special Housing Unit), but I think I wouldn't mind the solitary confinement. Learning all these rules of engagement ain't no joke.

I think twice. If I killed this Bitch, that would make two times she'd stolen my dreams and taken away my freedom.

I consider turning around and heading back to my cell. She had nothing I wanted to hear. And I damn sure wasn't about to give her an ounce of absolution.

"Sit. I won't stay long. I promise." I hesitate, but pull out the chair and sit.

I can't stop staring. "What do you want, Camille?"

"To tell you what happened."

I look around the visiting room, then lean in. "I *know* what happened. I went to jail and you did not." I sit back in my chair, cross my arms over my chest and roll my eyes. "What's left to say?"

"Plenty," she says. "To begin with, I had no intention of things turning out this way."

"Look Bitch, if you're feeling guilty, then go to the superior court and confess. Otherwise, we're done here —I'm not interested in your apology--"

Camille raises her right hand. "Oh no, you misunderstood me. I'm not here to apologize. I said I came here to tell you what happened. Explaining and apologizing are two different things."

"Whatever. You want to play semantics, you go right ahead. Either way, I'm not interested. If what you have to say does not include a confession or how you're going to get me out of here—then I don't give a fuck. Not about what *really* happened, or about you, Bitch." I stand up and glare down at her. "Fuck you."

"Fuck you, Monica," Camille shoots back evenly. "Fuck you for thinking you can have life both ways. Well you can't. And now the one time shit doesn't go your way, you want to have a fit and stomp out the room like a victim."

Just as I move to grab her and choke the self-righteousness out of her mouth, a CO walks by. I quickly step back.

"Is there a problem inmate?" The older CO stops and looks from me to Camille.

"No, Officer Winston. No problem." I slide back into my seat. He walks off and continues surveying the rest of the room.

Once out of hearing range, I say through clenched teeth, "Camille, first of all – this is not *the one time* shit didn't go my way. My entire life has not gone my way. Do you think I swung on a pole three nights a week because I had nothing better to do? No Bitch, it was to pay my tuition, because unlike you, my parents couldn't afford to.

"So don't pretend like you know me or what the fuck my life has been like, because obviously you don't know shit." I look around the room and lower my voice to a whisper. "And secondly, I *am* the victim, you crazy Bitch. You killed Marcus, and instead of you serving a fifteen year sentence, you went and got a fucking makeover and started a whole new life."

"And your point is?" We lock eyes.

"The point is, this isn't a game, Bitch. This is my life!"

"And like I said, you can't have it both ways, Monica. When it's going in your favor, it's a game. But when you're losing, then all of a sudden it's your life?"

"Bitch, what are you talking about, I can't have it both--"

"'It's not about the money. It's about feeling alive. The rush. Making shit happen from nothing. The thrill of getting away with it.'" Camille is staring at me. "Isn't that what you said?"

"No. Jacky said it."

"Yes, but you agreed," she says, almost indignantly. "You tried to beat me up when I dared question Jacky about it."

"Camille, this shit is not some fucking monopoly game. This is real life—*my* fucking life."

"Right, and when I asked you and Jacky about how what you were doing affected innocent people, *you* said that it was okay to do shit at the expense of others because, and I quote, 'In the real world there are winners and losers. If yo game is tight, you win. If yo shit is raggedy, then you lose.'"

My neck snaps back. I can't believe what I'm hearing.

"So, like I said – you can't have it both ways, Monica. It is what it is all the time, not just when it serves you."

I'm sitting here, trying to wrap my head around what this crazy Bitch is saying.

"I was trying to tell you, I didn't start off with the intention of things going this way." Camille slides her bangs behind her ear. She grabs the charm on her neck and rubs it as she speaks. And for a split second, I am expecting her to start rocking. But instead, she slides up in her seat and becomes very confident; I would even say, slightly irritated. "It just, sort of happened."

"You, completely lying on the witness stand is *just sort of happening?*" I roll my eyes.

"No. That was Zahra's doing." She waves her hand. "I'm talking about everything – the way it all came together."

I'm watching her lips move, but I stop hearing the words coming from her mouth. Is this Bitch serious? I mean, does she think I'm going to sit here and believe things just sort of happened? No, she lied and as a result, I was convicted of a murder I didn't commit.

"What do you mean that was Zahra's doing? Did she tell you to commit perjury?" I say it casually, but if she says yes, I have grounds for an appeal: misconduct. I'd get Zahra's ass disbarred.

"No, of course not," Camille replies, a scowl covers her face. "She simply stated that it was your word against mine, and only you and I knew the truth."

"And from that you got 'lie on the witness stand'?"

"No." Camille pauses. "But when I told her what happened I started by giving her background on our . . . history. After hearing how you stole Marcus from me, she said that God works in mysterious ways, and that maybe this was your time to get justice."

"Justice? Camille – that was high school!" I scream. The people sitting at the two tables near us turn and look at me. I pause, watching the stoic look on her face. "How can you believe that serving a fifteen year sentence is justice for taking your boyfriend in high school?" My head is throbbing. This is ridiculous.

"No, Monica, you took more than that. You see, if you had never interfered with our relationship, Marcus would be alive today." She rubs the charm on her necklace. "We would have gotten married, had two kids, and Marcus would have never gone to jail. He would have never turned into the monster he became. Our love would have taken him down a completely different road," Camille's eyes narrows. "But you were a selfish, conniving whore, and you ruined everybody's life: Marcus', Jacky's and mine - so now you are suffering the consequences."

Camille squeezes the charm. The corners of her lips inch up into a sinister snarl.

"You're crazy! You know that? You killed Marcus. Jacky was killed because she was trying to help your ass. I'm in jail because you lied and said I did it. You need to own your shit. What happened in high school doesn't give you a free pass to do what you've done as an adult."

Camille slams her hand on the table and leans in.

"Sure it does! You changed our entire trajectory, so now you're paying for your sins."

"And you?"

"Excuse me?"

"I'm paying for my sins. Since you were the person really responsible for all this bullshit, what do you get?"

"Restoration," she says with a smug smile.

"Restoration?"

Camille reaches into her purse, pulls out a 3 x 5 post card, and slides it across the table. "Yes, you heard of Job, haven't you? In the Bible?"

I'm reading the post card while Cam is talking. It's an announcement of a gallery exhibit. Camille has a show at the world-renowned Gavin Wright art gallery in SoHo.

"Job was a faithful servant of God. All of his worldly possessions, family, everything was taken from him as a test. But because he endured, stayed faithful--God restored him. A new family, ten times the wealth." She glared at me. "Restoration. This exhibit is God's way of honoring my faithfulness." She smiles. She juts her chin toward the push card. "With the popularity of the case, all the locals are obviously interested in seeing the pictures --"

"Wait, what? Pictures? What pictures?"

"Yes. I took pictures all weekend long. I documented every moment I could with my cell phone.

I didn't remember Camille taking pictures, but that's not to say she didn't.

"That's what I'm trying to tell you. It was instinctual for me to take pictures. And now, those photographs are being showcased at an art exhibit!"

"Bitch, did you document you smashing in Marcus' head?" I hiss.

Camille turns away from me. She scans the room.

All I can hear is swishing in my head. The temperature is rising in the room and this fucking jumpsuit feels like it's strangling me.

As hard as I worked to pay for undergrad so I could attend law school, and this Bitch has the audacity to tell me that my fate is to be on the other side of the law?

She's delusional. I'm watching her face and she's clearly checked out from reality.

"We all played our part, and things happened the way they were supposed to," Camille says evenly. "You just thought I was stupid." She smiles. "You underestimated me. And so did Marcus." She grabs her charm and rubs it slowly. Then she looks into my eyes and says, "But I showed you. Didn't I? I outsmarted you and now you're getting exactly what you deserve." She pulls the long piece of hair behind her ears.

"What I deserve?" I look around the room. "What I deserve? I've been working my ass off all these years, making all kinds of sacrifices so that I could become an attorney, Camille – not rot in jail for a crime I didn't commit."

I stand and glare down at her. "There's no way I'm going to sit here and listen to you try and ease your conscience with this self-aggrandizing psycho-babble about this is where I'm supposed to be. Fuck you," I spit those words at her, then turn and walk away.

CHAPTER NINETEEN

The Real

*"Wherever you fly,
you'll be best of the best.
Wherever you go,
you will top all the rest."* [22]

Camille

August 19, 2017   *2:00 p.m.*

I watch as Monica walks away from the table. Her orange jump suit flattening out her normally curvaceous bumps and curves. I shake my head and grab my purse, stand, and head for the glass cage at the entrance where the guards are. I slide my visitation pass through the slot.

Oh well, I tried. I tried to help her see her part in all of this. It didn't happen by chance. She had her hand in this ending.

The metal door swings open; I head down the long corridor to the outside, and board the old bright lime green school bus waiting for the six of us leaving before visiting time officially ends.

We make the drive down the long dusty road. A sixteen-foot fence topped with circular barbed wire line both sides. The bus wobbles as it crunches over the pebble-filled dirt road.

I reflect on my conversation with Monica. Nothing I can do now, but live my life. I tried to get her to see. Her anger and entitlement prevents her from taking ownership of what she set into motion.

---

[22] Dr. Seuss, *"Oh, The Places You'll Go!"* verse 10

I look out the window and watch a group of inmates playing handball up against a wall near the center of a long grey building.

I can't imagine spending fifteen years or the rest of my life in this god-forsaken place. But Monica should feel right at home with this seedy lowlife community.

I can't believe how much I wanted to be like her. Correction, how much I actually wanted to *be* her, because being her meant I'd have Marcus' love again.

I remember watching them from across campus using the zoom lens on my camera. I had purchased a special fast, high-powered sports lens with a shutter speed that promised to be powerful enough to "realize dramatic detail—from every bead of sweat and every pirouette." I hesitated buying it at first, but I know that description referencing the dance move was a sign from God.

I watched up close how she looked into his eyes, how she'd pout her ruby red lips, and have him practically begging her for affection-- affection that she'd give, but not before she teased and tantalized him into submission. The sports lens caught every move. I had hundreds of up close pictures.

Marcus loved it. Probably because he knew it would end with sex. I followed them a few times. She gave him head under the bleachers and in the equipment room. They mostly had sex in her dance studio though. It was their lair of sex and sin.

The first time I watched them I cried. It broke my heart to watch Marcus share the most sacred act of love with her. But the more times I watched them, the more I learned . . . how she bit her bottom lip, how she arched her back, the way she pumped her body and made Marcus explode.

I loved it. But I hated it. She was in control and it was powerful. But she was in control of Marcus and I didn't know how to break the spell.

So I watched her. I tried to become her. But I was too far away. Even with the zoom lens. I needed to get inside her head. I needed to know how she thought so that I could feel and think that way. These were the things that Marcus loved, and I needed to know everything, be everything. So, I followed her.

I noticed the only person Monica hung out with was Jacqueline Roberts.

Jacqueline was in Jack and Jill. Both our parents were very active members. Much to my mother's surprise and delight, I started to participate in more activities. I volunteered to work on the same events that Jacqueline worked on until one day she noticed me.

"Oh, hi. Thank you so much for staying after to help us clean."

"No problem. I don't mind."

"I'm Jacky, what's your name?"

"Camille. Camille Coleman."

"Candi Coleman's sister?"

"Yep." I roll my eyes. "The one and only."

Jacky laughed. "Oh, I'm sorry. I didn't mean to--"

"No worries. It happens all the time. People never really see me. All they see is a way to get to Candi."

Jacky stops packing up the decorations.

"Well now that's just silly." She says, looking into my eyes. "First of all, no offense, but your sister's not all that." I chuckle.

"But secondly, I only mentioned her because of the cotillion."

I roll my eyes. "Yes, I know." Jacky laughs and continues packing the boxes. "The debutante extraordinaire."

She smiles. "Well, thank you again for your help."

After that interaction, Jacky would come speak to me during our community service projects or tutoring the tweens. One day she invited me over her house.

"Hey. Not sure what you're doing this weekend, but would you like to come over and hang out?"

"Who all is coming over?"

Jacky chuckled. "Just you, if you come. Why?"

"No reason." I hesitate. "It's just. I don't get along with a lot of the girls at school." I grab the charm around my neck and rub it. Jacky looks confused.

"We attend the same school."

"Oh shit. I didn't know that." Jacky grabbed her burgundy cashmere sweater and slid it over her head. She pulled her long silky black hair out from under the sweater. She grabbed a grey scarf with burgundy stripes and wrapped it around her neck. "Well, I don't either. I really only hang out with one girl from school."

And that's where it all began.

Jacky would tell me things about Monica in passing. Things, most would consider harmless. She told me about her home life, and her aspirations to become an attorney.

But it was the other things that I lived for. Things like, "Monica loves this color lipstick. Or, Monica just bought that dress."

I'd go back and buy the ruby red lipstick, the dress, the perfume.

I'd stand in the mirror and practice pouting my lips.

After a while, I became an expert at applying makeup. I had a brand new wardrobe. I just never wore them out in public.

But I had mastered everything I could. When Marcus realized that he loved me and not *her*, he'd come back to me. And when he did, he'd never leave me again. I'd give him everything he ever needed, and he'd never fall into the arms of another woman again.

The bus comes to an abrupt stop. The other visitors grab their belongings and exit the bus. I grab my purse off the seat and stand, waiting my turn to exit.

I look back in the direction of the building where Monica was. I tried to tell her . . . how it all came together. But she'll never know the truth now. She'll never understand how life just happened—I could tell she didn't believe me, but it did.

Monica

The library can't open fast enough.

I spend the entire Sunday stewing over Camille's visit. Her statement that I thought she was stupid and underestimated her fucked with my mental all night.

That entire visit and everything about it has me vexed.

Her words, her looks, her brand new life . . .

I can't believe the nerve of that Bitch! She actually looked me in my face and told me this is where I was supposed to be.

We will see.

I request copies of my trial transcripts and spend the next three weeks combing through every sentence, every exhibit. As I'm reading, I'm reliving it like it was just yesterday.

I flip through the pages of the transcript. Remembering the trial. Trying to see where it all went wrong.

It didn't matter. I was in prison, doing a fifteen to L for a crazy Bitch.

I spend every waking moment in the library reading, highlighting.

Something's not right.

I take the pages of photos of Marcus' bedroom taken the night of his murder that I'd gotten from the evidence file and lay them across the huge library table.

"Got dammit! That Bitch!'

Monica

September 4, 2017   *9:30 a.m.*

"Chula," I say, approaching a Samoan-looking Mexican. "I hear you need some help with your case?"

We're out on the yard. She's standing near the handball court. Obviously just standing there for shit's sake because that big Bitch couldn't run back and forth up a court to save her life. She'd drop dead of a massive coronary.

"Yeah? Who told you that bull shit, SA?" She looks me up and down.

I throw my hands up. "Look, no worries." I back up. "My home girl said you was cool people and asked me to do her a solid. I ain't looking for no trouble." I turn and walk away.

"Hey, Boricua. Slow your roll." She walks over to me. She nods to the right, and I follow her over to the barbed wire fence. "I don't like people all up in my shit. And a Bitch is getting old. I forgot I asked East L.A. to put a word in for me."

"Yeah. No worries," I say. "I ain't trying to get caught up."

"Nah. I hear you." She smiles, showing two missing front teeth: A big one, right in the front, and the incisor tooth to the left of it. And that, right there—is what I'm trying to avoid. Beat downs in prison usually lead to missing teeth, organs, and limbs. "But yeah. So, you can take a look at my case. What's it going to cost me?"

"For sure." I look around. "I hear you got the hook up with the iPhones?"

She nods. "I can get the iPhone 7. That Bitch got all kinds of features."

"Yeah, I bet. But check this out. I need to get *my* iPhone smuggled in. Can you do that?"

Her eyebrows go up. "Ah shit. I don't know about that."

"That's what I need, Chula. I need access to the photos on my phone. I can get my people to get it to your people." I look at her and shrug like it's no big deal. But deep down inside my stomach is doing flip-flops because I need to get to those pictures.

"Let me see what I can do."

"Cool. In the meantime, I'ma need you to put in a request for all your court transcripts. I'll start reading them as soon as you get them to me. Cool?"

"Cool. Hell yeah."

It takes less than a week to get my phone. My younger brother drops my phone off at a gas station three miles from the prison on his way to visit me. Two days later, the Samoan-built Mexican delivers it. She tapes it underneath the library table.

I spend two hours going through my pictures until I find it.

Pictures of me and Marcus standing in the center of his apartment, both wearing one of his baseball jerseys. It was one of those rare happy days. We had set the timer and posed for the picture. We stood back to back, each of us holding up a bat like we were about to hit a homerun.

I smile. That was when Marcus had just gotten released from prison. Before he started hitting me. Before I realized what a mean bastard he had become.

I swipe left. And there are the two bats leaning in the corner of the room!

It takes the rest of the week putting together my hypothesis. I had only taken one logic and reasoning class, but I applied everything I had learned into making my case.

I spend the rest of the week putting together my hypothesis. I had only taken one logic and reasoning class, but I applied everything I had learned into making my case.

I take on little Tabitha's case. She works in the business office and has access to a printer. Her payment is printing out the pictures from my phone.

At the end of the week, I make a call to Detective Morales.

EPILOGUE

From the Eye of the Beholder

CHAPTER TWENTY

Double Jeopardy

"Oh, the places you'll go! There is fun to be done!
There are points to be scored. There are games to be won.
And the magical things you can do with that ball
will make you the winning-est winner of all.
Fame! You'll be as famous as famous can be,
with the whole wide world watching you win on TV." 23

Camille

September 28, 2017   *5:30 p.m.*

It's the night of my exhibit and I'm feeling alive.

Everything I've longed for has culminated into this night. Recognition as a social issues photographer, my parents respecting and supporting my career choice, and being featured in an exhibit versus moderating it. I know from personal experience that many careers have been jump started from one exhibit. This could be the start of mine.

There's a knock at my dressing room door.

"Yes?"

"Hello, Camille."

I turn to face the voice. "Detective Morales." I turn back to face the mirror. "To what do I owe this pleasure?" I pucker and apply Mac Ruby Red to my top lip. "You don't strike me as the art exhibit type." I pause and turn to face the detective.

"Congratulations," the detective replies. He walks over to the wall and leans back. He lights up a cigarette.

"Please, Detective. The smoke."

---

23 Dr. Seuss, *'Oh, The Places You'll Go!'* verse 24

"My bad." He smashes the cigarette out on the floor.

I roll my eyes. "I don't have much time. How can I help you?"

"This won't take much time," he says, pulling out a manila folder.

I don't turn to face him, instead I watch him in the mirror. "I went to see Monica in jail."

I smirk. "So did I. I hope your visit went better than mine." I apply the lipstick to my bottom lip.

"I don't know about better," He says. "But it was interesting." He opens the folder. "She's been doing her own investigating and has a theory that I'd like to run by you, if you don't mind?"

I pause for half a second. "Sure."

"Great. Thank you." He positions himself so that he's standing directly behind me, looking at me in the mirror. "Apparently, Ms. Lopez has spent countless hours combing through transcripts, witness testimony, and trial evidence to try and prove that you set her up for Marcus' murder."

I apply a thin line of black eyeliner on my left eyelid. "Yes Detective, that was her position during the trial." I pause and look at him. "What's new?"

Detective Morales smiles: a slow, sensuous smile.

"What's new is this."

He lays three photos on the vanity table in front of me. One is marked exhibit number four – it's a picture of the empty corner of Marcus' room. The other is a picture of the same corner with two bats in it. And the last picture is of Monica and Marcus, standing in the center of Marcus' living room. They are standing back-to-back, both wearing one of his baseball jerseys, and holding a bat in the hitter's stance—elbows at a ninety-degree angle, hands clutching the neck of the bat. The bats are at a forty-five degree angle, justly slightly behind their heads.

"Exhibit four is a picture of Marcus' room. The corner is empty."

I look up at Detective Morales. "Monica was able to get these pictures that show there were two bats in that corner: a wood and a metal one. And here is another picture of them holding those two bats." He's looking me in the eyes. "Monica's theory is that you killed him with the wood bat, and planted the metal bat, framing her for Marcus' murder--"

"Detective Morales," I say, grabbing my mascara. "I'm going to tell you like I told Monica. 'We all played our part, and things happened the way they were supposed to.'"

"What does that mean?"

"Exactly what it sounds like." I put my mascara down, and swivel around on the chair to face him. "Things happened the way they were supposed to. Monica isn't ready to accept that yet. But I suspect after a bit of time, she will come to realize it's true."

"So you're saying Marcus was supposed to be murdered, Jacqueline was supposed to get killed, Monica was supposed to spend the rest of her life in jail, and you were supposed to capitalize off of it all?"

I smile. "I'm going to explain it to you like I tried to explain to Monica. But she refused to listen."

"I'm listening."

"Good. Because I need you to understand," I say, almost in a whisper. "We *all* played our part. I didn't go into this situation with the intent of framing Monica. Things just . . . happened."

Detective Morales' eyebrows arch up into a question.

"My attorney has informed me that I cannot be tried for Marcus' murder again, so I have absolutely no reason not to tell you the truth, Detective. But I am on a tight timeline, so, if you don't mind?" I swirl back around and start applying a second coat of mascara.

"By all means." He waves his hand.

"Thank you," I say. "As I was saying, we all played our part. Let's take you, for instance." I look up into the Detective's eyes. "Your part was supplying Marcus with drugs." The detective's lips tighten. "Oh, yes. He told me all about the stolen evidence."

Marcus didn't mention the detective's name, but I figure this Morales guy must be the dirty detective. Why else is he pursuing this case after it's been tried and settled?

"He told you I gave it to him?"

"You're missing the point," I say, looking into his eyes. "The point is, we *all* played a part. You, me, Monica, Jacky . . ."

"And?"

"And, none of us went in with the intentions of things turning out this way. Not you, not me – certainly not Marcus or Jacky. That's what I was trying to explain to Monica. But she wouldn't listen." I pick up my makeup brush, swirl it around in the foundation and apply it to my forehead and chin. "But things happen for a reason."

"What do you think the reason is?" Detective Morales says, folding his arms across his chest.

"Restoration," I say smiling. "Tonight is *my* night. The first of many. God is honoring my love and dedication to Marcus." I apply makeup to my right cheek, then my left. "I was faithful to him, you know? The entire time." I pause, staring into the mirror. "Heart, body and soul. I waited for him. I knew he would come to his senses and see . . ." I vigorously apply another coat of powder.

"And, because of your . . . faithfulness . . . God is restoring you?"

"Yes." I slam the brush down on the counter. "Like Job, his faithful servant. He was restored ten-fold." I smile into the mirror.

"Too many things lined up. Too many things fell into place." I pick up a small brush and begin applying nude eye shadow. "It was God, ordering my steps. And I did my part. Everything fell neatly into place."

"Like what?"

I smile, finally able to tell my side of the story.

"Well, for starters, Marcus being drunk and me arriving in time to take him home," I say to the detective. "I had played it over and over in my head, a million times. And I knew the day would come when I'd have a second chance to prove my love to Marcus." I look up in the mirror. "Do you know he said I didn't love him because I would not have sex with him before we were married?"

"So, you got a second chance?"

"Exactly!" I nod; excited that he understood what Monica could not. But of course she could not, she never thought about me and Marcus' love. She came and took what wasn't rightfully hers.

"All I needed was the right opportunity, and it came the night I went to the club. I loathed that seedy carnal den of sin. But the fact that I agreed to go and Marcus ended up needing me to take him home was one of those things that lined up.

"But I don't understand, if this was your second chance, why did you kill him?" I stop applying my makeup and take a deep breath.

"Marcus tried to defile me. I can't believe he'd try to violate me, knowing I was giving him what no man, besides my husband, was entitled to have."

"Defile you? What did he try to do?"

"To have anal sex," I say between clenched teeth. "That may be the type of bestial acts that Monica participates in, but not me. I'm no whore—and he wasn't going to desecrate my temple."

I apply mascara to my top right eyelashes.

"I was terrified and angry at the same time, Detective. He was so strong. And I was certain he was going to force himself inside me. The look on his face was manic and depraved. I was so embarrassed.

"Then, I became uncontrollably angry. It's like he was spitting at my virginity. Laughing at my humiliation. That's when I snapped."

"And you hit him?" He says. I nod.

"When Marcus staggered into the bathroom I heard him say, 'Worthless Bitches . . . think they too good . . . don't nobody want you' and all I wanted to do was shut him up. Silence his vile, disgusting, trap. I rushed into the bathroom; his back was facing me. And with everything in me, I swung! There was a loud crack" I stare into the mirror, remembering the blood splattering everywhere.

"And then?"

I blink.

"And then he fell to the floor." I place my hands in my lap and look at them. I chuckle. I look up, "The words stopped. And for a brief moment, I felt exuberant.

"He wasn't worthy of my love Detective. I had no intention of killing the man I planned on spending the rest of my life with, my husband, the father of my children. But I would not be disrespected. I'd had too many years of that--the embarrassment the last two years of high school. People asking me what happened to me and Marcus, then snickering. And then in college when we crossed paths because of Jacky. It made me sick. The disrespect ended that night."

"I see." Detective Morales says. "And the girls? You said everything lined up. Did getting the girls involved---did that just happen as well?"

"Actually, yes." I say. "After standing there for several minutes the fog and anger started to dissipate. Reality started to seep in, and I started to panic.

"Calling the girls, getting them there to help me figure out what to do next, it was perfect. They were the reason I was in this situation in the first place. I would have never gone to that club on my own."

"Wait, you called the girls?"

I purse my lips in a smug little smile.

"God." I say. "Jacky had called me earlier from her trap phone. Her regular phone had died. I dialed the last number in my phone."

"And that's why the DA didn't find a call from you on her phone." He said.

I tilt my head and raise my eyebrows. "Bingo."

"So Monica never burst in the room in a jealous rage."

I shake my head. "I honestly believe she burst in the room because she knew what Marcus was capable of." I brush my hair. "I think she thought I was weak and she was coming to save me."

"When she saw that he was dead, she handed me the bat and told me to take it down to the car."

"But you dropped it down the chute, knowing we'd find it."

I wink. "She had no idea I had switched out the bats and taken the wood bat down to my car. When I got outside and didn't see Jacky I grabbed the wood bat out of my trunk and put it in the trash bag so they would think it was the metal bat."

"So, Jacky never made it upstairs?"

"Never." I say. "She pulled up just as I was replacing the bat. I couldn't have timed it any better."

"I see. And . . . so, what did you do with the bat?"

"It's in a landfill somewhere. They dumped it and a bunch of Marcus' things in dumpsters in different boroughs across the state."

I smile at the detective. "You see? It all lined up."

The detective scratches his goatee. "Okay. What did you do with the cocaine?"

"I flushed it down the toilette at some car wash I found on Google." I say.

"You what?" The Detective shouts. "When?"

"The day after my arraignment. One more day and my car would have been towed. I know it was favor."

"And you flushed both bricks down the toilette?"

"Yep. I used my key to punch a hole in the bricks and slowly poured the white powder down the toilette. I had to push the button every two to three minutes to clear the bowl.

"God gave me closure." I whisper. "I honestly believe it." I look directly at the detective. "The love of my life and my best friend were gone. I needed to say goodbye. God spoke to me. He told me to free their souls. So, as the powder swirled around the blue liquid in the toilet, I imagined me standing on a boat at sea."

I close my eyes, remembering.

"The first brick was Marcus' remains, and I'm pouring his ashes out to sea. Behind me is Ms. Bernadette, Cory, my parents and the priest—all of us are dressed in black. The priest genuflects as the ashes dissolve into the blue abyss below . . . 'Into your hands, I commend his spirit, oh Lord . . .' I flush the last of the contents and grab the second brick." I lift my hand as if I'm pouring out ashes.

"This time, the boat is filled with Jacky's mom, dad, and brother. Several athletes and celebrities stand behind the family. As I pour her ashes, tears flow. I thank her for being my only true friend. I flush and flush and flush. And cry, and cry, and cry."

I open my eyes. The detective is staring at me.

"So, you see? It all worked out as it was supposed to."

I stand, and straighten out my skirt. "No evidence linking you to Marcus." I walk toward the door. "And Monica, well. She created her own storm, now she's upset because it rained. She finally got what she deserved. And me." I open the door and turn to wait for the detective. "Well, here I am." I waive my hand high in a swooping motion toward the galleria.

The detective grabs the photos off the vanity and walks toward the door. He pauses as if he's about to say something, shakes his head instead and says, "Congratulations on your show, Ms. Coleman. All the best to you."

"Thank you, Detective Morales."

CHAPTER TWENTY-ONE

Most Likely to Succeed

"You're off to Great Places!
Today is your day!
Your mountain is waiting.
So . . . get on your way![24]

Camille

September 28, 2017   *7:30 p.m.*

"Ladies and gentlemen, please put your hands together in welcoming the featured artist of tonight's exhibit," the curator announces.

The crowd gathers, clapping in anticipation of my arrival.

I make my way into the gallery in my black stiletto heels, striding purposefully into the waiting crowd. Cameras flash.

To the right, are poster-sized yearbook photos hanging from fish wire. They are pictures of each of us at the peak of high school: Monica gliding three feet off the ground in a dance move; Marcus swinging a bat, that's just about to connect with a baseball; Jacky, in mid-sentence at an academic decathlon, and me posed behind a camera taking a picture of some random subject.

Up five feet and to the left are *'Most Likely To'* headshots. Monica's caption reads: 'Most Likely to be on a Reality Show,' Marcus' reads: 'Most Likely to Land a MLB Contract,' Jacqueline's says: 'Most Likely to Marry a Celebrity,' and mine says: 'Most Likely to Ace the SAT.'

---

[24] Dr. Seuss, *"Oh, The Places You'll Go!"* verse 1

I grab the hand of Victoria Rengal, my boss at the gallery and then turn and blow an air kiss to Jason Kincaid, my publicist. Before I can take another step, a classmate from La Guardia steps in front of me, leans in and snaps a selfie.

As I step down into the main area of the gallery, eight feet high photos of Monica swinging on a pole, Marcus' mug shot, Las Vegas lights, Monica behind bars, and Jacky and Marcus' crime scenes line the center of the gallery.

I take my place in front of the glass podium.

Monica

September 28, 2017   *7:37 p.m.*

"Hey Lopez, ain't that the chick from your case?" an inmate says.

I look up at the TV just as Camille turns her head. Her short bob swings around and covers her cheek. The camera freezes on her face: her head is tossed back; she's smiling brightly--her fire engine red lips juxtaposed bleached white teeth—are a stark difference to her chillingly cold black eyes.

"*All alone, whether you like it or not. Alone will be something you'll be quite a lot.*"[25]

"What?" the inmate says.

"Nah, I've never seen her before in my life." I turn and leave the rec room.

---

[25] Dr. Seuss, *"Oh, The Places You'll Go!"* verse 27

Camille

September 28, 2017   *8:00 p.m.*

I smile brightly for the camera.

It's my time. My moment. But I'm not present.

Right now, all I see is Monica walking hand in hand with Marcus, hugging and kissing in the quad; I see the girls looking at me and laughing; I remember the pain I've felt over the years.

I blink a couple of times, willing myself to enjoy every minute of this moment.

Then I see Marcus standing in front of the bathroom mirror, and me swinging the bat, watching as he falls slowly to the floor, the blood forming around his head.

I see Monica in her orange jumpsuit, behind sixteen-foot barbed wire fence. And I smile and say to myself:

And will you succeed?
Yes! You will, indeed!
98 and 3/4 percent guaranteed.[26]

---

[26] Dr. Seuss, *"Oh, The Places You'll Go!"* verse 32

www.ingramcontent.com/pod-product-compliance
Lightning Source LLC
Chambersburg PA
CBHW060108260626
47160CB00005B/1833